CW00555888

IN THE STICK OF TIME

E. LOWRI

First published July 2023

ISBN: 9798851378775

Independently published

"Time is the most powerful force in the world; it heals, steals, and gives. It ripples through the lives of every living thing and bends to no one's will. The only little control we can have is to use it wisely, respect its inevitability, and understand both the greatness and limitations that brings" - *E.Lowri.*

For mum and dad.

PROLOGUE

Alicia lived a life of excitement and impulse until an unexpected event shattered her spirit, and changed her way of living life. In adventure she now only sees danger. In spontaneity she now only sees uncertainty. Alicia finds comfort in the familiar; control in the safety of routine. Never allowing herself or her son to stray far from the well-trodden path; never pushing beyond the boundaries of her walls. But despite always sticking to a carefully crafted plan, she is about to discover that life can still be alarmingly unpredictable. One day she is forced to take a path she never expected to find, and the consequences fracture forever the very foundations of her world and others.

CHAPTERS

CHAPTER 1
THE SAFE PATH

"It is when we all play safe that we create a world of utmost insecurity" - Dag Hammarskjöld

As the first light of the day emerges so too does Alicia. Rubbing the sleep from her puffy eyes, she pulls back the heavy hallway curtains. Golden streams of light flood in giving a sparkle to everything it touches. Alicia glances into the orange-tinged antique mirror and touches her silky smooth, ginger hair; each strand shines beautifully from the warm glow of the morning sun. Her fingers caress the ends of the ginger waves. For a moment she mulls the idea of keeping the long locks loose. With a deep inhalation of breath the decision is made: she pulls her hair back into a tight pony-tail. Patting out a few stray bumps, she assesses the sleek-backed look and then heads into the kitchen.

The kitchen looks pristine. Not even the bright sun seeping through the large windows manages to uncover a single speck of dirt. The room shows surprisingly few signs of age considering it is an offspring of the 1980s, with its cream cupboards bedecked with brown accents and dark shiny worktops sculpted some 30 years ago. Alicia flicks on the kettle and pulls two china mugs out of the cupboard; one is adorned with the letter 'A' and the other with the letter 'R'. Leaning against the counter waiting for the water to boil, her sleepy gaze surveys the room until her eyes settle upon a picture hanging on the wall. The image of a man with his arms wrapped around her stares back at her.

The kettle starts to rattle like a train on the track as steam begins shooting out in an upwards spiral towards the picture. Similar to a sun-filled sky becoming overcast, the steam clouds eventually reach the man's face, and Alicia watches as his bright eyes fade away beneath the carpet of grey. The kettle announces its work is done with a sharp beep causing her to abruptly exit her thought. She looks down at the two mugs and shakes her head in frustration. She grabs the mug embellished with the letter 'R' and places it back in the cupboard. Alicia stirs the tea clockwise and counts to four. She stirs the tea anti-clockwise and counts to four again. The sound of metal meeting porcelain echoes throughout the stillness of the kitchen as she taps the teaspoon four times on the edge of the cup to dispose of any further drips of tea. She walks over to the large wooden table and sits on one of the eight vacant seats, taking care to place the mug precisely in the centre of the coaster. One further coaster lies across from her but aside from this the table lays bare.

Alicia studies the array of polaroid photos on the adjacent wall that decoratively border a large mirror. The familiar face of the man can be seen amongst some of the images along with a young curly- haired boy. Other photos contain a smattering of laughing faces seated at the very table where she now sits. She looks around at the empty chairs whilst gently sipping her tea. Turning towards the display of photographs once more, she catches sight of the woman in the mirror; an immaculately presented lady: hair sleekly tied back, shirt with all the right creases in the right places, necklace polished to perfection, nails manicured. Yet her insides feel the opposite; a mess of emotional knots growing tighter each day. Alicia clutches her stomach for a moment as if trying to hold something in.

The curly-haired boy from the photo suddenly bursts through the kitchen door with such gusto Alicia almost spills her tea. She quickly returns her mug to the safety of the table. The boy's arms are proudly laden with provisions for the day ahead: a ball, a small fishing net, and an empty jar.

'Mum! Let's go. It's finally sunny', he excitedly declares.

'Well, good morning to you too, Patrick', she responds in a slightly exaggerated tone of surprise.

Her eyebrows slowly rise like a pair of birds taking flight as she watches him place the various objects down on the table with a loud clunk. He brushes his hand through his thick brown hair. Alicia watches his curls get flattened then pop up once more like perfect little springs.

'What? Oh', he says, noticing Alicia's stare and realising he owes her a reply.

Patrick spots a fresh bunch of bananas on the counter and proceeds to grab one.

'M-morn-i-ing', he mumbles whilst shoving a half-peeled banana into his mouth.

'Right then', Alicia says with a sigh. 'Usual place?'

Her tone suggests it is a fact more than it is a question. Patrick nods unenthusiastically. *Usual boring place,* he thinks to himself.

'Good', she replies. 'Make sure you have everything you need. Spare socks, plasters, bite cream, water—'

Patrick quickly swallows the last bite of banana, eager to interrupt.

'It's the *same* walk we do every week. Nothing ever happens. I never need extra socks!'

Alicia shrugs and gestures for him to go upstairs. Patrick, not wishing to waste anymore time inside, disappears obediently up to his bedroom to obtain the requested items. It was the first day of the school summer holidays, and he was keen to make the most of not being stuck in the classroom.

Alicia heads over to the sink to wash the mug; cleaning with such vigour that it literally becomes 'squeaky' clean. The high-pitched squeaks as the cloth meets the shiny china fill the room. Even the 'A' printed on the side of the cup is lucky to survive.

Whilst she waits for Patrick she cannot resist turning her gaze back towards the picture on the wall. She closes one eye and places her thumb in the air covering the face of the man in the photo. She holds this pose for a second or two, observing the now solitary figure of herself in the picture. Swallowing heavily, she lowers her hand and allows her arm to flop down by her side.

Rapid thuds can be heard echoing through the small house as Patrick runs back down the stairs and enters the room, clutching a blue bag adorned with a map of the world. Little red ink dots are scattered across the map representing all the places he wishes to go. A single green dot placed in Wales represents where he has been. Once again Alicia's train of thought is broken, and she turns to face a red-cheeked Patrick. She looks at the bag he is holding high in the air like a trophy, a subtle gesture he is ready to go.

'Has that green dot grown?, she enquires.

'Yeah remember I went to Cardiff Castle with school', he replies.

'Socks, plasters.... whatever else is usually in this. 'It's all here. Let's go!', he says holding the bag even higher.

He clumsily begins to cram the jar, fishing net and ball into the bag. Without even stopping to zip up the bag, he hurries out through the back door and into the garden. Alicia grabs her raincoat, two water bottles, some headache tablets and her keys. She picks up her mobile phone and touches the screen but it remains blank. She looks over at the wall socket and notices that it is switched off. Tutting and rolling her eyes, she reaches over and turns the switch on. She places the phone back on the side to charge, before joining Patrick who is stood waiting on the path. He is looking longingly towards a neglected red 1960s MG car parked in their driveway. It is clearly well-used and once loved.

'You know Mum, I really wish you'd let me drive that', he says with an air of confidence.

Alicia stares at the car; as her eyes study the once loved family jewel, her mind begins pulling her into a scene filed deep away in her memories.

- - - -

A man is driving a car and badly rapping a song at the top of his voice. He glances over at her as she sits in the passenger seat. His eyes are filled with delight from the obvious amusement and annoyance he is causing her. She notices a bright light suddenly shining on his face, and then the light begins to fill the car - as if the sun is rising up ahead, except the sun is setting.

- - - -

Alicia shudders as she shakes herself from the memory and returns to the present day.

'You're 11 years old - I think you can wait a little longer. Besides, you can turn the key in the ignition but I doubt the car will take you anywhere anymore', she says.

Patrick tilts his head back and lets out a groan of disappointment.

They make their way down the stone path that runs through the modest but pretty garden; similar to the car it has a look about it that suggests it too was once much loved. A Willow tree sways in the breeze, its branches rise up and down as if waving them goodbye. Alicia shuts the creaky gate behind them and they begin briskly walking up the grassy hill that adjoins the garden. The house is surrounded by rich, green countryside with no other nearby houses in sight. Alicia had always loved the stillness and peace; as if they had a slice of the world all to themselves.

Alicia looks up at the blue sky noting that it is under threat from a large looming cloud. She feels a sudden chill in the air causing a shiver to surge down through her body from head-to-toe. She keeps walking but her eyes remain fixed on the cloud. *Something feels odd,* she thinks.

'Did you feel that chill just now?', she asks Patrick.
He looks back towards her with a confused expression on his face.

'No it's warm', he scoffs.

He glances at the raincoat she is wearing.

'I'd be even hotter if I was in that', he says.

As they reach the hill's summit, Alicia begins to slow and takes some deep breaths. A pang of tightness creeps into her chest, the kind you get when your body demands more oxygen than it can take. Patrick however is unaffected by the steep climb and gestures for her to hurry up as he begins his speedy descent down the other side.

'Alright! Alright! For someone bored of the same place you're sure keen to go!?', she says breathlessly.

'Well as long as I'm going *somewhere*, even if it is the same place. I can't stand being in the house. Nothing ever happens here does it?', he calls back.

'Some people may say that's a good thing you know?'

'Well I've never met those people. But how would I? Go to the same places all the time. School, home. School. Home. School...'

'Patrick one day you'll understand why sometimes the safe and predictable life is the happier life.'

'Is that what dad thought?', he replies without missing a beat.

Alicia averts her gaze away from Patrick and looks over at the cluster of trees towards the base of the hill; an impressive eclectic mix of tree species, their branches and leaves rustle in the soft wind like an ocean of foliage.

'Oh look, Patrick. A deer!'

Alicia raises her arm and points towards the trees. Patrick hurries down the final incline.

'Where!?', he shouts.

Alicia smiles and pauses for a moment watching her son enthusiastically search for the deer she never saw, grateful that the subject has shifted. He ducks and weaves looking through the openings between the trees as he tries to catch a glimpse of the elusive creature. He eventually gives up, shrugging his shoulders and running his hand through his messy hair which seems to have expanded from the heat and sweat. He joins Alicia once again, who is now casually meandering down the hill which leads into an open meadow, her breath now finally caught.

'You know when I said I was bored? That doesn't mean you're boring', he says.

A hint of guilt flashes across his face.

They continue to walk across the meadow which is a shimmering carpet of yellow, as hundreds of dandelions bask under the light of the sun. An old stone farmhouse can be seen in the distance. No doubt once a bustling family home, it now sits in ruins with its insides as exposed to the elements as its outsides are.

'But you could be more fun', he continues.

Alicia lets out a loud laugh.

'So I am neither boring nor fun? What an interesting thing to be', she muses.

'Well you can be fun. Like with dad we always played games and did stuff.'

Alicia glances up at the sky, the once looming cloud has now vanished with no trace. She places her arm around Patrick as they continue to walk. Her eyes fall upon the ruined farmhouse again. *So many reminders,* she thinks to herself. She feels her brain pulling out another memory from her mind's library.

- - - -

Patrick is crouched, hiding behind a crumbled wall of the farmhouse listening intently to Alicia as she calls out for him.

'Patrick! Oh Patrick! Where are you!?', she calls dramatically - a little too dramatically, causing him to snigger.

Alicia detects the uncontrollable sniggering and looks over towards the wall with a smile across her face.

'Oh where are you?', she asks.

She begins to sneak around the side to surprise him.

'Aha!', she yells triumphantly tapping Patrick on the shoulder from behind, making him jump to his feet.

Seconds later a further 'Aha!' is heard, this time it is a deep male voice. A man appears behind Alicia causing her to jump.

'Nice one dad', Patrick says through giggles.

'Yes very funny Rhys', Alicia says turning towards him.

He puts his arm around her and laughs loudly.

- - - -

The midday sun now takes centre stage in the sky and beats its heat down on Alicia who is sat by the edge of the stream on top of her now defunct raincoat. She watches Patrick who is rummaging around the cusp of the woodlands in the distance. His left hand clutches an array of different-sized sticks which he has carefully chosen. The sky is an endless blue. The stream mirrors the blue above as it reflects the beauty of the sky back up to itself. Nothing breaks the peace except for some distant birdsong, the babbling water and Patrick talking to himself. He heads back towards Alicia holding his treasure trove of sticks tightly. Alicia leans over and grabs a stick she has spotted near where she is sat.

'You know mum, and I shouldn't really help you out as — well because I don't want to lose, but maybe you wouldn't always lose poohsticks if you didn't always pick the first stick you see.'

He places the heap of sticks carefully into a pile on the grass.

'It's all about the right stick', he says proudly with his hands resting on his waist. 'A racing car driver doesn't just pick any old car.'

Alicia lets out a chuckle.

'Yes but today I think this stick feels like the winning one!', she says waving it in front of her as if it were a wand. 'It looks a bit like a wand actually', she says as she swooshes and flicks the stick once more as if conjuring a spell.

Suddenly there is a loud splash, as if something had jumped into the stream next to them.

'What was that?', she says craning her neck to look behind Patrick towards the stream.

'I don't see anything', he says as he turns to examine the water.

'How weird, I could have sworn I heard—'

'Anyway', he interrupts. 'All I am saying is *that* stick is the first one you saw so you just grabbed it.'

'Well....maybe it was meant be the first one I saw?'

Patrick frowns realising that he has nothing further to say. Alicia pushes herself up off the ground and spends some time brushing away bits of grass and dirt from her clothes. Patrick waits for her impatiently, tapping a stick on the side of the old stone bridge.

'You don't even have any dirt on you', he says finally.

'Just making sure', she responds.

Alicia makes her way up to join him. Her hand glides softly over part of the bridge where the initials *R.S* are amateurishly engraved; she has done this so many times her eyes no longer need to guide her hands to the spot. Alicia turns to Patrick.

'See, we still play games. We do this one all the time.'

'Well I do like winning all the time I guess', he responds.

'Right then, on 3? 1, 2, 3.'

They release their sticks and watch them plummet into the ripples of the stream with a gentle splash-splash.

'But I wish we could do other things together', Patrick says suddenly, as he watches the sticks disappear beneath the bridge.

Alicia stays where she is for a moment and continues to look down at the stream as Patrick runs to the other side of the bridge. She wipes away the softest of tears before joining him. They stand in silence. Patrick's eagerness morphs into confusion as the sticks fail to reappear.

'Um... well no sticks means no winners - so I guess no losers either!', he says rallying his eager spirit once more.

'They must have just got stuck', Alicia concludes.

'Come on let's grab another two', she says.

They each choose a stick from the pile and once again take up their positions on the bridge.

'1, 2, 3', they say together.

The sticks are dropped into the stream. Alicia and Patrick watch them disappear before running to the other side of the bridge once again. No sticks reappear. They look at each other in confusion.

'Well—', Alicia says hesitantly. 'I suppose we should investigate?'

Patrick immediately runs down to the edge of the stream.

'But don't go in the water!', she calls after him.

Alicia makes her way more cautiously to the edge of the stream too, but on the other-side of the bridge. Hunched over like a gargoyle she tries to see signs of the wayward sticks in the dark underpass.

'I can't see anything that could block them. Although I can't even see them to be honest', she declares.

'The water is moving fast though. Look at that duck go!', Patrick calls back.

He watches a duck happily allow itself get carried along with the flow of the current, floating underneath the bridge and moving beyond Patrick's line of sight.

'What duck!?', asks Alicia.

'Um... the duck that just floated under the bridge.', Patrick says with an eye roll. 'You'll see it appear on your side in a minute.'

Alicia looks bemused; no duck emerges from beneath the bridge. She waits for another several seconds for one to appear.

'Patrick there is no duck', she responds with an air of annoyance.

Patrick, who had been down on all fours straining to see under the bridge, jumps back up on his feet and rubs the grass from the palms of his hands. He glances towards the trees still keeping an ever watchful eye for the deer. He sighs. *No deer. No sticks.*

'Mum if you are trying to be funny I don't think this counts.', he says still rubbing his hands together trying to remove the imprints the grass has left on his skin.

'What?', she replies.

Alicia battles gravity and manages to get herself upright, shaking her head at her son's confusing duck joke. She heads back up onto the bridge.

'One final try?', she asks grabbing a stick from the pile.

Patrick nods. This time they drop them into the water without counting to three. Once again they find themselves waiting in vain. No sticks reappear.

'Well I admit it is a bit odd.', Alicia says after a spell of silence.

'A BIT odd!? In the entire history of poohsticks this has never happened', he says dramatically.

'Well—'

'Come on we have to go under the bridge!', he declares.

Patrick hurries back down towards the stream.

'Wait a minute Patrick! You are not going in that stream! It is wet, and cold, and unclean', Alicia orders

'The water will only reach my ankle and I can see the bottom of the stream. It looks like the water we drink', he responds completely undeterred by her authoritative tone.

Alicia hesitates for a moment. Patrick is already dipping his shoe in the stream.

'Wait!', she bellows.

Patrick freezes mid shoe-dipping. The sound of her son's voice informing her that they never have fun together echoes in her mind. She looks down at the stream and then looks at her son's expectant face. She resolves herself to her fate.

'Fine I will do it. You just stay there! I mean it, you stay there', she tells him sternly.

'I could go in. I have spare socks', he says.

'Just stay there.'

Alicia begins to roll up the bottom of her trousers, taking care to ensure each trouser leg is rolled to the same height. Patrick rolls his eyes. She then takes off her shoes and places them neatly at the side of the bridge making sure they are lined up side-by-side perfectly. She squirms as she feels the grass touch the bottom of her bare feet.

'Why do you do that mum?', he asks.

'Do what?', she replies looking around for clues as to what he could be referring to.

'Make everything neat. Or match. Or pack like a gazillion things for a walk like today.'

Alicia is genuinely surprised at the question and takes a moment to consider her answer.

'Well Patrick I guess... I guess it's how I feel safe. In control. How I...', she looks up at the sky for a second before raising her hands in the air shouting: 'how I cope with the never-ending unpredictable chaotic mess of life.'

Patrick and Alicia stare at each other in awkward silence.

'I see', he says rubbing his chin.

Feeling a little coy about her sudden outburst of truth, Alicia clears her throat and straightens her already straight shirt. She pats Patrick's arm as she passes him on route to the stream.

'I think I'll enter this side', she says. 'It looks less.... bumpy.'

Patrick shakes his head and rolls his eyes once more. *Bumpy?,* he thinks to himself.

She gingerly edges down into the stream and flinches from the sudden feel of the cold water enveloping her feet. The flinching continues all the way to the bridge as she feels every stone and every leaf that touches her skin.

'More towards the centre. That's where we always drop the sticks', Patrick instructs.

Alicia chooses to stay to the side of the bridge with one hand pressed against it to keep her steady. She takes a moment to allow her eyes time to adjust to the dimming light as she goes further underneath. As she stares at the water she knows something is not quite right but it takes a minute or so for her brain to tell her what it is.

'What on earth?', she whispers to herself.

The water directly under the middle of the bridge is still. There is no movement at all. Yet the water all around the sides moves freely. She stares perplexed for a moment before dismissing it as nothing more than a trick of the light, or rather a lack of clear light. Glancing around, she sees no sign of any sticks or anything that could have blocked their passage through.

Suddenly realising how cold her feet are, and how much she is disliking this damp adventure, she begins to quickly move through the arched passageway. In her haste she trips on a rock, almost falling flat on her face in the middle of stream; but she successfully avoids such a fate, managing to steady herself by flapping her arms like a flightless bird when she realises the walls of the bridge are no longer within reach. Giving herself several seconds to recover, she then continues to make her way out towards the other side, resolute in the fact that poohsticks was over for today.

'No sign of them', she calls out to Patrick. 'We must have missed them in this bright sunlight - trick of the eyes or something.'

She glances up and notices it is overcast, with a noticeable chill in the air.

'Patrick?'

Alicia clumsily scrambles out of the stream and begins looking around for him.

'Patrick? Where are you?'

She turns in circles looking for him. No sign of him on the bridge. No sign of him by the stream. No sign of him near the woods.

'PATRICK! This is not funny!'

CHAPTER 2
LOOKS LIKE RAIN

"Life takes us by surprise and orders us to move towards the unknown — even when we don't want to and we think we don't need to". - Paulo Coelho

Alicia begins running back-and-forth across the bridge, along the edge of the stream and then into the meadow. She stands still for a moment and then begins spinning around, looking in all directions unsure which one she should go in. *How can he have got away so quickly,* she thinks. She begins to feel short of breath as panic starts to seep into her lungs and tighten them with fear. She tries to take a deep breath in and out, but her whole body abruptly freezes in astonishment as she watches her breath turn to mist in the air.

'How can it be this cold so suddenly!?', she says to no one.

As she watches the mist evaporate it reveals a steady stream of smoke behind it in the distance. Her eyes and her brain battle each other as she tries to compute what it is that she is seeing: the smoke is coming from the chimney of the farmhouse. The chimney that, a mere few moments ago, lay in pieces on the ground. Alicia stares unblinking. The outline of the stone building is clearly visible beneath the puffs of smoke. No mist forms around her mouth as she stops breathing momentarily. She squeezes her eyes together and reopens them, hoping that what she is seeing is all in her imagination; but alas the complete farmhouse still stands in all its glory. She raises her hands to her shaking head. *Impossible,* she thinks. Then she notices something else; no dandelions. Then another peculiarity; no leaves on the trees. She clutches her stomach with both her hands, and bends over readying herself to be sick.

'This makes no sense!', she wails.

Alicia lets out one more cry for Patrick before dropping to her knees, still clutching her stomach. Throwing her head back, she looks up at the grey sky and tries to quell the irrational thoughts racing through her brain. *Did I knock my head? Did I pass out? Has someone taken him?* Suddenly she hears something; a distant voice perhaps. She leaps to her feet.

'Patrick?'

Turning towards the bridge she can make out the figure running towards her.

'Patrick! 'Where were you!? When I tell you to stay put, you stay put! I was worried sick', she fumes.

His eyes are wide and his cheeks glow with excitement. Alicia pulls him into a hug, although frustration still pounds inside of her. After a few seconds he wriggles free from the hug, and begins talking at pace.

'I wasn't the one who went somewhere. You were', he tells her.

'What are you talking about?, Alicia says. 'Look I think mummy is overtired let's go back home.'

She rubs her forehead as if trying to release a genie to whisk her back home, and away from this confusion.

'NO!', Patrick unintentionally yells.

He looks a little embarrassed by his sudden eruption.

'Er.. sorry', he mumbles. 'But you have to listen. Come with me!'

He hurries back towards the bridge and pauses at the edge of the stream, staring back eagerly awaiting Alicia to join him. He waves his arms at her impatiently. She reluctantly follows him, still rubbing her forehead but now hoping it will rub some sense into her brain. He points up towards the sky.

'You see the clouds?', he asks.

Alicia nods. Her brow furrows as she tries to understand the significance of what she is seeing. She deduces it must be some freak weather occurrence. There is a sudden splashing sound which causes her to turn abruptly, only to discover that Patrick is wading through the stream towards the bridge. She gasps, horrified.

'What are you doing Patrick? Get out of there!'.

'You need to follow me', he says.

'But—'

'You must!', he says with much more force this time.

Alicia clutches her forehead once more, unsure which of them is behaving more oddly. Is her mind playing tricks? Patrick calls out to her again, and with much huffing and puffing she slowly begins to follow.

'Come on', he says impatiently.

Alicia hesitates as she teeters on the edge of the stream and quite possibly insanity. Only now that she is considering placing her feet back into the stream does she realise how freezing cold they are; her toes, already tinged with blue, recoil at the thought of their imminent fate. She submerges one foot in the water and lets out a faint whimper.

'Just put them both in. Don't think about. Sometimes it's better to think less and do more - isn't that what dad said once?', Patrick tells her.

'Whatever that means', he continues with a shrug. 'But it feels like a good moment to say it'.

A smile flashes across Alicia's face but it is soon replaced with a grimace as she begins to tread through the water. Her foot catches on a stone causing a stabbing pain to surge through her toe; she lets out a short, sharp cry as she stumbles towards the wall of the bridge. Steadying herself with her hand against the wall she looks up just in time to see Patrick step into the centre of the stream underneath the bridge. He vanishes in front of her.

There is a delay between Alicia's brain processing what her eyes saw. After a minute of standing frozen to the spot like a statue, she bursts into life.

'Ahhhhhhhhhhh!'

She lunges towards the spot where he vanished in a desperate hope that a weird trick of light meant he is in fact still stood there. Feeling disorientated Alicia begins to sway but the walls of the bridge are no longer in reach.

'Mum...'

She feels nauseous and begins to swallow hard to fight the urge to be sick.

'Mum...'

The sound of Patrick's voice filtering through the fog of her bewildered brain helps her to regain her balance and steady herself. She moves quickly from beneath the stone arch and follows the breadcrumbs of his voice.

'Patrick?'

Now oblivious to the discomfort of her feet, her adrenaline-fuelled limbs move with ease and nimbleness through the water and over the many stones. Alicia spots Patrick standing on the grassy bank grinning at her, his dimples on full show and framing his smile perfectly. Before she can open her mouth and air her annoyance at this soggy situation she finds herself in, he points up towards the sky.

'Look at the sky now', he says.

She haphazardly climbs out of the stream and turns her face towards the sky. It is blue with no clouds in sight. It is noticeably warmer too. No longer satisfied with rubbing her forehead, she begins to rub her whole face with both of her hands; she squeezes her eyes shut and gives her cheeks a quick slap, as if this would somehow wake her from a weird dream. *Were they really clouds I saw moments ago,* she thinks to herself. The logical part of brain screams *no*, but her memory of what she saw does not falter.

'Woah! I think this is some sort of… weather-changing bridge', Patrick says thoughtfully whilst scratching his chin.

Alicia looks over at the farmhouse in the distance which sits in ruin again. She looks across at the trees in full bloom once more.

'Um...', she says.

'Let's do it again!', Patrick announces.

He hurries back towards the bridge; slipping, sliding and creating splashes with such zest his clothes become heavy with water.

'What!?', calls Alicia.

Patrick does not hear her, or perhaps chooses not to.

'Could you just stay put for a moment', she orders angrily.

The splashes he was creating suddenly stop. Silence fills the air. *Oh no. Not again,* Alicia thinks to herself. She feels deliriously bewildered.

She rushes to the other side of the bridge but Patrick does not emerge. She then rushes back to the other side; Patrick does not emerge there either.

'Oh—!', she yells, resisting the urge to say anything stronger.

Her legs carry her back under the bridge but her mind remains fixated on the farmhouse - images flash between the ruins, and a fully functioning house complete with a smoking chimney. Alicia heads towards the exact point she saw him disappear with no real idea why or what relevance this may have. She is fuelled by instinct and adrenaline. Alicia walks underneath the grey masonry and emerges out from the other side of the bridge. Patrick is standing on the grass several feet away. He is stood very still with his back to her.

'Patrick what is it?', Alicia cries as she hurries next to him.

She feels goosebumps breakout across her skin like a rash as her body starts to shiver. She folds her arms tightly in an attempt to keep warm. *What's up with this weather,* she thinks as she looks up at the now overcast sky. Her feet tingle from being wet and cold.

She traces his gaze to the farmhouse in the distance. Patrick continues to stare intensely; his mouth wide open, his eyebrows squeezed together. He seems unperturbed by the cold chill that fills the air.

'Wait. A. Minute', he says slowly. 'There is something different about that farmhouse. Someone has lit the fire. The chimney is smoking!'.

He whips around to face Alicia.

'Oh thank goodness. You see that too. And… what about the fact it's also no longer a ruin?', she says.

Patrick's mouth widens once more as he slowly moves his gaze from Alicia back to the farmhouse.

'I knew there was something else different', he cries.

With barely a second to dwell on how the farmhouse has magically rebuilt itself, Alicia feels a tap-tap-tap on the base of her back. She screams, causing Patrick to let out a high pitched shriek too. They both turn around quickly to see who is standing behind them.

A young boy with disheveled strawberry-blonde hair stares back at them with a toothy grin on his face. His clothes are tinged with dirt: a white/grey shirt with unevenly rolled-up sleeves, and brown trousers that are too short for him. The the hems are frayed no doubt from a time when they must have been too long. Holding this whole outfit together is a simple pair of braces. His hand clutches a woolly hat and a coat he clearly has no desire to wear but was forced to take out with him.

'Hi', the young boy says. 'I'm Merlin.'

'Ah!', Alicia yelps and takes a step backwards almost losing her footing. 'What? Who? Mer-Merlin?'

Patrick looks over at Alicia perplexed by her reaction.

'Erm are you okay mum?'

She begins muttering to herself and pacing the grass.

'M-e-r-l-i-n. Like the Wizard?', Alicia mutters.

She glances at the farmhouse and then up at the cloudy sky.

'So you did this?', she says turning towards the young boy briefly before turning away again, and continuing to pace.

Patrick and Merlin exchange a quick look and both shrug their shoulders. An unspoken mutual understanding had been reached; neither boy knew what was going on. Patrick watches Merlin try to catch a fly, only to slap himself in the face and fall over.

'Um..... mum?', Patrick calls to Alicia but his eyes remain fixed on Merlin.

Merlin jumps back up off the ground, looking a little confused as to how he ended up down there.

'No. No. No. Don't be an idiot. Merlin is a fictional character. Isn't he? But what on earth is happening right now', Alicia continues to mutter.

She shakes her head in exasperation.

'I need to lie down', she concludes.

'I think it's just a boy called Merlin', Patrick tells her quietly.

'What?', she replies.

Alicia walks back to join Patrick. She watches Merlin try to wipe mud off his bottom. He smells his muddied hand and then skips off back towards the sound of laughing voices somewhere in the distance.

'Ah. Yes. Of course', Alicia says.

Her cheeks fill with colour, as if someone has just taken a paint brush and with one swift stroke painted them red.

'Patrick I think mummy is having some sort of breakdown.'

She glances back at the farmhouse.

'Or maybe we are having a joint one', she says putting her hand gently on his shoulder.

The voices in the distance begin to come closer. Alicia spots a couple of children running across the meadow but both are too preoccupied with chasing one another to spot her and Patrick. She turns to face Patrick who seems oblivious to the children.

'Let's go look at the farmhouse!', he says excitedly.

Patrick begins to walk away from Alicia. She runs in front of him blocking his route and raising her arm up, summoning him to stop.

'Don't you think this is all a little too odd?', Alicia exclaims. 'We need to think. Or have a sit down.'

She rests a hand on her waist and uses the other one to massage the front of her head. She glances back at the children who seem to be on a trajectory towards the woodlands.

'And don't you think something about them seems... off?', she continues.

Patrick watches the children chasing after each other; he shrugs at Alicia, unsure what she means.

'Just Something about the way they look. The way they dress', she says.

Patrick crosses his arms, rubbing his hands up and down his bare skin that is now feeling the affects of chilly air.

'It's cold', he says.

Alicia goes to speak but no words come out; all words escape her. She does not have a plan nor an explanation. She looks over in the direction of the hill and wonders if they should just head home.

'Come on', she says. 'Let's head to our house.'

'What about my bag?', Patrick asks.

They both look around. No sign of the bag. No sign of Alicia's shoes either.

'Well maybe the kids took them, I don't know', she says dismissively, feeling increasingly tired.

'Let's just get home Patrick.'

They make their way through the meadow and begin their climb to the top of the hill; both feel grateful for the warmth this exercise brings. Alicia deeply regrets having no shoes to wear. Every so often she winces in pain as her foot encounters a stone. The feeling of her bare feet walking over grass and dirt makes her skin crawl; she tries to silently count her breaths to calm her nerves. Patrick listens to the squelch of his wet socks in his shoes.

'We could do with those spare socks right now', he says.

Alicia glances over at him with a raised eyebrow, but she resists the urge to respond. They continue their uncomfortable walk back up the hill. *Everything just doesn't seem quite right,* Alicia thinks to herself. *Even the trees seem off - different.* As they reach the hill's summit they both come to an abrupt stop. They stare down at the base of the hill with their eyes and mouths wide open.

'The Willow tree has gone', Patrick cries.

His eyes move beyond the now vacant spot where the tree once stood.

'And our house is gone too!', he wails.

Alicia drops to the floor; her energy drains. She looks down at the now empty piece of land in disbelief. *How? Why?* After a minute, Patrick joins her and sits cross-legged on the ground, staring at the void below and mindlessly plucking pieces of grass from the ground

'This is just weird', he says matter of factly.

Alicia looks at him with surprise.

'Bit of an understatement that Patrick', she says.

Alicia's hands begin to tremble from shock.

'Quack.'

'What on earth is that!?, Alicia cries.

They both turn their heads in the direction of the sound, and see the mystery duck from earlier waddling up to them.

'I told you there was a duck!', Patrick says, mesmerised by the feathery friend.

The duck casually plonks itself down several feet from them, as if it had been waiting for their arrival. Alicia can tell that Patrick is already making plans to keep it as a pet. She looks at the creature with suspicion. The duck ruffles its feathers, and studies them intensely for a moment before deciding it is safe to nap. It tucks its head into its chest and sleeps.

Patrick commences plucking bits of grass; his eyes remain on the duck. He bites the edge of his lip, deep in thought.

'We should go back under the bridge. That's where everything changed', he says.

Alicia sits in silence, initially dismissing the idea. But as the minutes tick away, no other course of action makes sense. They could walk the several miles to town. *Knowing our luck the town has vanished,* she thinks. Patrick leans into Alicia, his body flinches as he shivers. She puts her arm around him and tries to provide him with some warmth. Then, shaking her head in defeat, Alicia gets to her feet.

'Come on. Quick! Let's go', she demands. 'To the bridge.'

Patrick gets up, brushing a multitude of freshly picked grass from his trousers. He feels a little surprised she has chosen to go with his plan. He moves quickly before she changes her mind.

'Should we take the duck?', he asks.

'What? Absolutely not', Alicia says.

Patrick looks back at the creamy white bird and bids it a sad farewell. It tilts it head to the side and watches as they disappear.

Arriving at the stream's edge, they glance at each other with apprehension. There is no sign of the children. The air feels still and silent, except for the sound of the water.

'Hope this ruddy well works! Whatever *this* is', Alicia says. 'Let's make sure we do everything exactly the same as we did before. This way Patrick.'

Alicia grabs Patrick's hand and they take the increasingly familiar journey through the stream. Patrick feels Alicia's grip on his hand tighten as they pass underneath the arch. They slowly emerge from under the bridge and each take a moment to bask in the sun's light, and the sudden warmth that greets their skin. Panting heavily Alicia climbs up the bank and looks up at the blue sky and towards the ruined farmhouse.

'Look!', says Patrick. 'My backpack.'

He runs over and picks up the bag and places it in front of Alicia, as if he has just found the treasure after a long hunt. She begins straightening out the bottom of her jeans and then starts to pick bits of grass and dirt off her clothes. *It's okay,* she tells herself. She breathes in and counts to four. She breathes out and counts to four. Alicia wants nothing more than to get out of these dirty clothes and wash them. *Get some control back,* she thinks. She can hear Patrick excitedly chattering in the background but her mind feels too frazzled to make out the words he is speaking. Her foot suddenly catches on something.

'Ow!', she exclaims.

She lifts up her foot and examines the underneath for signs of damage, before looking on the ground for the cause of problem. She reaches down and picks up a stick. Never in her life has she ever been able to re-identify a random stick; they all look the same to her. Until now. This stick has a smooth, velvety grey look to it with a round knotted piece of wood in the middle like a clock face minus the hands. It was the first stick she had picked up ready for their poohsticks debut of the day. *How did it get on the grass?,* she thought. She grabs Patrick's backpack and shoves the stick in with no idea why she is doing this, just an overwhelming feeling that she should. She looks around at the grass. *My shoes!* She heads over feeling relieved to see the familiar objects, and pulls them onto her feet.

'Patrick, I... I want you to promise me you won't go near that bridge until—.'

'Until what?'

'Until I have t-time to think.'

'Think?'

'Yes. Think.'

Patrick looks puzzled.

'Hmm okay', he says kicking a stone into the river.

'But I wouldn't recommend thinking much. I want to go back under there soon.'

He crosses his arms defiantly. Alicia frowns and rubs her forehead again.

CHAPTER 3
THE VANISHED

"To ask the right question is already half the solution of a problem". - Carl Jung

Rolando sits at the wooden table in the kitchen, frantically trying to wipe away evidence of the tea he spilt. A large wet ball of tea-soaked tissue grows rapidly as he adds more to it. Satisfied he has now cleared his mess, he jumps to his feet and stuffs the evidence into the nearby bin, blissfully unaware of the trail of tea drippings he is leaving behind him. He sits back down and lets out a big breath before picking up a cookie and taking a bite out of it. The cookie crumbles everywhere. He throws his head back in disbelief. Looking out the window he spots Alicia has nearly finished hanging the washing out on the line. He quickly scoops up the stray crumbs and shoves them all into his mouth.

Alicia returns to the kitchen and immediately spots the mess; the empty cup with drip marks down the side, the crumbs of dismantled cookie framing Rolando's mouth, the damp tissue sticking out of the bin like a tongue. She smiles.

'Oh don't worry Rolando. Patrick makes far more of a mess sometimes!'

Rolando blushes and laughs feebly.

'Well it's just your house is so tidy these days', he says. 'Not that I'm saying it used to be messy.'

Rolando shifts in his seat awkwardly. Alicia smiles at him. She knew what he meant but decided not to respond to it. Since Rhys had gone things had changed. She knows exactly where every little thing in her house is, and nothing is ever out of place.

Alicia hands Rolando another cookie and pours him a fresh cup of tea from the pot. She mops up the rogue crumbs with a mini dust pan and brush.

'Where is Patrick anyway?', Rolando asks.

'Up in his room. No doubt plotting some wild adventure', she says.

Alicia thinks back to the bridge escapade. Her head feels heavy with unanswered questions.

'Are you okay?', Rolando asks.

'Oh yes', she says shaking her head.

Rolando looks at her with scepticism. Alicia avoids his gaze and sips her tea. Rolando had been Rhys's best friend, and she had known him for 15 years. But his familiarity did not make the prospect of confiding yesterday's peculiar shenanigans any easier. They continued to drink their tea in silence for a minute or two. Alicia takes a moment to reflect on how well her friend is looking. His skin glows with health, his jet black hair looks silky soft, his dark eyes sparkle with mischief. His teeth are a good three shades whiter than they have ever been. Alicia feels a great satisfaction in seeing her friend doing so well. It has, she thinks, been long overdue.

'So', she says.

Rolando waits eagerly for the next words; it takes Alicia a few false starts to deliver them.

'Yesterday something peculiar happened', she finally says.

Rolando straightens up in his chair with a sense of anticipation.

'Are you okay? Is Patrick okay? What happened?'

'Yes we came to no harm', she says as she glances down towards her feet which suddenly begin to throb, no doubt from their recent excursion.

'It...it's very hard to describe or even explain.'

Rolando places his cup carefully back on the coaster and leans towards Alicia.

'Since Rhys left us I know you don't have many people you feel you can talk to', he says gently, a tinge of his lost Spanish accent seeps through. 'But me and Ali vowed to be here for you and Patrick. So just start saying words and we can puzzle all this together.'

He smiles softly and leans back in his seat. He picks up his tea and begins drinking it again.

'Well', she says as she closes her eyes. 'What would you say if I told you that by walking underneath the bridge down by the stream, you actually walked through some sort of weather changing, farmhouse regenerating portal-thing?'.

Alicia opens her eyes and finds Rolando choking on his tea.

'Oh gosh are you alright?', she asks.

'W..w...went.....wro....ng....way', he splutters whilst gesturing to his throat in case there was any doubt where the problem lies.

After a few minutes Rolando manages to bring his airways under control. He looks at Alicia open mouthed, his eyes streaming from coughing too much. Unsure what to say in response he sits in silence for a little longer and fiddles with his wedding ring.

'I'm just going to message Ali', he says.

Alicia begins to laugh manically as the comedic insanity of what she just said takes hold of her. Rolando flicks between staring at Alicia and his phone, as he texts a message to Ali:

Come here now.

He places his phone back down, his eyes are now solely fixed on Alicia. Her laughter suddenly turns into one big sigh. She leans on the table and throws her head into her hands.

'I know how odd it sounds', she mumbles through her palms. 'But whatever happened to me, well it also happened to Patrick'.

She emerges from her hand cocoon and looks earnestly at Rolando. He leans over and pats her on the arm.

'I know things have been hard lately—', he says.

'No. I mean, yes they have. But I am telling you I walked under the bridge and the next thing I was in... a different place. Well the same place. But different.'

'And at what point did you wake up?', Rolando says with a nervous laugh.

Alicia sighs and nestles her head in her hands again. Rolando glances up at one of the polaroid pictures which contains an image of Rhys and him dressed in their finest Welsh rugby kit. He smiles at the faces staring out at him. He thinks back to the first time he ever met Rhys, and chuckles inwardly as he remembers how odd he thought he was. Rhys seemed so naive, as if he had been living under a rock until he turned 22. The summer he had met Rhys they had bonded over their love of music. He remembers how Rhys was completely mesmerised by his Walkman, having never seen or even heard of one before. Rhys had spent all his days that summer listening to every kind of music he could find. Rolando smiled at this resurfaced memory.

Rolando looks back towards Alicia. He feels a deep responsibility to look out for Rhys's family now that he is no longer here to do it himself.

'Alright. Show me', Rolando says to Alicia.

She looks up at him; the relief on her face is instant. She immediately stands up and begins grabbing her keys and coat. Rolando stands up too and glances at his phone but there is no new message. He places the phone in the back pocket of his jeans, and follows Alicia out into the hall.

'I'm going to the Bridge with Rolando. Stay here please', she calls upstairs to Patrick.

Alicia ushers Rolando out of the house before Patrick has any time to protest. They begin the familiar walk up the hill, only this time it is Alicia who is storming ahead and urging Rolando to hurry up. Rolando wheezes and groans; vowing never to eat biscuits again as he wipes beads of sweat from his forehead.

They reach the edge of the stream in record time; even Patrick would have struggled to beat them there. They stand at the edge staring towards the bridge.

'Er... so now what? We go in the water? I'll get wet', Rolando says.

'It's only the depth of your ankle. Look, I have spare socks if needed', Alicia replies.

She pulls two pairs of rolled-up socks from her coat pocket. Rolando looks at them in amazement.

'Do you just walk around with extra socks all the time?', he asks.

Alicia chooses not to hear this question.

'Actually there is an easier way to show you that something odd is going on', she says.

Alicia spots the last few sticks left on the side from yesterday. She picks up two and hands one to Rolando. He looks at her perplexed.

'What we gonna do? Duel?', Rolando says chuckling a little at his own joke.

'Pooh sticks. You know? A stick race?', she says.

'Ah', says Rolando, nodding his head before realising it still makes no sense to him.

He slowly follows Alicia onto the bridge, looking around as if waiting for someone to jump out and shout 'gotcha!'. Alicia explains the aim of the game to him quickly.

'Right, on 3. 1, 2, 3', she says.

They drop their sticks into the stream and watch them get whizzed away by the current. They race to the other side and wait for them to reappear.

'Ah look I won!', Rolando triumphantly announces pointing towards the two sticks floating out from beneath the bridge.

'What? No', Alicia says rubbing her forehead.

'Yes, that is clearly my stick in front', he says.

'No Rolando, I mean this isn't what happened. They shouldn't reappear.'

'Erm... are you sure you played this before?', he says with amusement.

Alicia starts throwing further sticks into the stream and rushes to the other side, only to see them all reappear. Raising her arms and shoulders in a dramatic shrug, she about turns and runs down to the bank of the stream. She throws her shoes onto the grass and enters the water. Rolando follows but stops short of going in.

'What are you doing Alicia!?', he shouts.

'Go wait the other side of the bridge, and watch what happens', she calls back.

Rolando decides it is best not to argue and does as instructed. As he heads to the other side of the bridge, Alicia waves and grins manically at him before going underneath. Rolando awkwardly waves back and takes up his position, straining his neck to spot Alicia coming through. Within seconds she emerges from under the bridge, and they both stare at each other stiffly. Each of them looks confused but for very different reasons.

'Well... that's very good', Rolando says as he massages the back of his neck with his hand, unsure what to do or say.

Alicia looks around her; the sky is still blue, the air is still warm. She scrambles out of the water and rushes to spot the farmhouse in the distance. It remains a crumbled ruin.

'Why isn't it working?', Alicia says aloud but to no one in particular.

'I think you should go home, put your feet up and just rest for a few days', Rolando says gently.

Alicia scowls.

'But—'

'We can talk again after you have rested some more', Rolando interrupts.

He puts his arm over her shoulder and tries to coax her away from the water. She eventually ceases to resist. She pulls on a fresh pair of socks, and finds her shoes which unusually had not been left neatly on the side. They head back to the house in silence. Both of them remain deep in their own thoughts. Rolando occasionally glances over at Alicia with the same look a doctor may give to a newly admitted patient.

'Just to check, you didn't hit your head or anything yesterday?', he asks.

Alicia has no energy to speak, choosing instead to just shake her head.

As they reach the house Rolando informs her he will check in tomorrow. She enters the house and calls out for Patrick. No response comes. She perches on the stairs, rubbing the back of her shin which aches from today's sudden burst of activity. She calls for Patrick again but still no answer comes. She pulls herself up and heads to his bedroom, the only messy room in the house. Maps, books and puzzles are strewn across the floor but there is no sign of their owner. *He wouldn't go back on his own,* she thinks. Alicia spots his sketch book laying open on his bed; the open page contains a colourful drawing of a bridge with sunshine on one side and clouds on the other. *Yes he would,* she concludes. She looks around the room once more and spots that his rucksack is missing. Slamming the sketchbook shut she throws it back on the bed and hurries out of the room. Grabbing her coat once more she rushes out the door; and perhaps for the first time in a long time, with no spare socks.

Rolando pauses at the end of the driveway, he pulls out his phone and begins to text Ali:

Weird things going on here. Did you get my last message?

He hits send, and looks back at the house. The door swings open and he sees Alicia march down the garden path, failing to shut the creaky gate behind her. She seems oblivious to the fact that she is being watched.

'I ask that boy to do one simple thing. To. Stay. Put', she furiously mutters to herself.

She assumes he must have been hiding somewhere, the woods perhaps, until she and Rolando had left the coast clear for him. She shakes her head in annoyance and curses her own naivety at thinking he really was just quietly playing upstairs.

Rolando tilts his head back and looks up to the heavens, as if waiting for some kind of divine intervention. None comes. He decides to follow her, but chooses to stay inconspicuous. Not far behind Rolando a man appears, he raises his hand to his mouth as if he is about to call out to Rolando but upon noticing that he is surreptitiously following Alicia, the man decides to say nothing and chooses instead to follow Rolando. He too decides to stay inconspicuous.

Alicia, so determined in her quest to find her son, never once looks behind her. Rolando, so determined in his quest to follow Alicia, never once looks behind him. The man following Rolando looks everywhere: back, forward, and to the side as he tries to find clues as to where on earth they could all be going. The sun bounces off the man's bald head; he touches the warm skin with his hand and hopes that come tomorrow it doesn't resemble a tomato.

Alicia reaches the bridge and much to her disappointment there is no sign of Patrick. Rolando quickly ducks behind a solo tree, an ideally positioned lookout point. He sucks in his belly noting the leanness of the tree trunk. The man behind Rolando begins to panic, suddenly feeling exposed with nowhere to hide. He throws himself flat onto the grass and remains still, watching Rolando and Alicia. She heads up onto the bridge and suddenly feels a surge of nausea rise up through her body as she spots Patrick's abandoned backpack. She rushes over to it and picks it up. As usual it is unzipped. She rummages through it; the only item that appears to be missing is the grey stick she had shoved in there yesterday. She wonders if there is any connection between the strange looking stick and the strange occurrence with the bridge. *Whoever has heard of a magic stick. It's ludicrous,* she argues with herself. Her rational brain fights for air as she glances down at the stream wondering if somehow he had vanished; if somehow the bridge had 'worked' for him. *Whatever 'worked' actually means,* she thinks. With no sign of Patrick she feels there is no other choice but to once again take the ridiculous walk under the bridge. She reassures herself with the thought that at least this time Rolando is not here to witness the madness.

Rolando watches as Alicia kicks off her shoes, and paddles towards the bridge. He kneels down on the ground and strains both his back and neck to see as far under the bridge as he can but he can no longer see her, or any sign of movement. He rushes down to the stream and tries to peer under the bridge.

'Alicia', he calls.

He waits and listens. There is no sound except for the gentle babble of water.

'Oh for goodness sake!', he exclaims.

Rolando awkwardly pulls off his trainers and falls into the stream with a high-pitched yelp. The man in the distance raises up from the ground as if doing some graceful yoga pose.

'What the heck?', the man mutters to himself.

Rolando gets back on his feet and looks down at his sodden clothes in a state of shock. He brushes back his damp hair and heads towards the bridge, shaking the water from his hands. He spots Alicia standing deadly still underneath the bridge with her back to him. She stares at the small round pool of water in the middle; it is definitely not moving unlike earlier. The water around it continues to flow by gracefully, totally undeterred by the strange phenomenon that is happening right in the centre of it. This small round area of the water is as still as the moon's surface. So enthralled by what she is seeing, she remains oblivious to the figure of Rolando moving towards her. She steps into the still part of the water. Rolando watches her vanish.

'OH.MY.WORD', Rolando cries.

He rushes under the bridge. An impish grin appears on his face. *Was she right - is this bridge magic?*, he thinks to himself with a pang of childlike excitement. In his haste he falls over once more, his foot catches on a rock. He clambers up again, and chooses to stay to the side of the bridge, using the wall to prevent him from falling yet again. He shuffles through the underpass with his back firmly pressed against the side, but is slightly blinded by the excess water that splashed into eyes. As he feels the wall of the bridge come to an end his eyes begin to work again and adjust to the light. With his arms wide open in jubilation, he begins to giggle as he heads towards the grassy bank.

'Oh wow!', Rolando says. 'Everything feels so different!'

'What on earth are you doing?', the man calls out.

Rolando looks around and tries to locate the source of the voice. He locks eyes with the bald man who is standing there looking back at him.

'Ali?', Rolando says. 'How did you get here?'

Rolando observes the familiar figure of Ali, stood on the bank with his arms folded; a frown covers his face. His biceps bulge through the sleeves of his t-shirt which reads 'BE HAPPY'; something that Ali was currently failing to be.

'I walked', Ali replies. 'Come here, give me your hand and I'll pull you out.'

Rolando moves towards Ali who stretches his arm out towards him, showing off his new tattoo of a dragon wrapped around his wrist. As Ali pulls him back up onto dry land, Rolando looks around and feels a jolt of disappointment.

'So I am exactly where I was to begin with', he says to Ali quietly.

'When you text to say weird things were happening, I didn't think you meant that *you* were the weird thing!', Ali says with a half smile, half frown.

'But you must have seen Alicia go under there', Rolando says gesturing towards the bridge. 'And she has... well vanished'.

Ali looks at the bridge and then looks at Rolando. He repeats this gesture about three times.

'Well, now you come to mention it.... where is Alicia?', Ali asks.

'I don't understand. I went under the bridge exactly like she did', Rolando says indignantly.

Ali clears his throat, hinting he is waiting for an explanation about what is going on.

'Come on', says Rolando putting his arm round Ali. 'Let's sit down and I will fill you in on my afternoon.'

CHAPTER 4
CHANGING TIMES

"Courage is not simply one of the virtues, but the form of every virtue at the testing point". - C. S. Lewis

Alicia stands on the bridge calling out Patrick's name. A steady train of mist funnels out of her mouth as the cold air meets the warmth of her breath. Whilst tightly gripping the front of her coat, her eyes sweep the area trying to seek out the figure of her runaway boy. As fear tightens its grip on her thoughts, so too does her hand's grip on her coat. She remains unsure what is real and was is not.

'Somethin' the matter?', a man calls out from behind her.

She gasps and whips around to greet the stranger coming towards her. A man with a striking carpet of bright white hair and mesmerising topaz blue eyes smiles at her as he joins her on the bridge. He walks with a slight limp but is able to move swiftly enough. The white hair is deceiving though; Alicia deduces that he must not be much over 30 years old.

'Sorry didn't mean to startle ya', he says apologetically.

'I-I'm trying to find my son Patrick. Eleven years old, curly hair - I think he may have come this way? Although I can't be sure', she says, looking around once more.

Will raises his hand in a gesture of reassurance.

'Ah well, kids come and go in these parts all the time. Always playin' around. He'll be round 'ere somewhere - and perfectly safe I may add', he says.

Alicia nods feeling strangely reassured by the man she has never met before.

'That bein' said, it is unfortunate he is off gallivantin' when there is an incomin' snowstorm on the way', the man continues. 'I'm Will by the way', he adds.

'I'm Alicia.'

She forgets herself for a moment and goes to shake his hand before pulling it back dramatically.

'Hang on! A snowstorm!?', she wails.

Alicia looks up at the heavy clouds that look ready to burst. Will looks Alicia up and down paying particular attention to her clothing. No shoes, rolled up trousers, and a thin strange looking coat; he had not seen a material quite like it before.

'They'll be turnin' blue', he says pointing at her bare feet. 'Where are ya shoes? Or are they missin' with Patrick?'

He lets out a little laugh to try and break the tension. It does not seem to work. It was not his finest joke, he reflects.

Alicia looks down at her poor embattled feet. They have had a hard couple of days. She feels rather embarrassed realising how odd she much look.

'They are rather cold, yes. I regret not bringing them with me. Why didn't I?', she says tapping her forehead with her palm.

'Where did ya come from?', Will asks.

'Oh we live in the house just over the hill. The one with the Willow tree', she replies.

Will looks at her, deep in thought.

'Er there is no house over that hill. Or Willow tree come to think of it', he says.

'Oh—', Alicia stutters, remembering her vanishing house.

'Come now', interrupts Will. 'I think it's best we get ya somewhere warm. I'll take the horse out to look for ya boy. It'll be much quicker than goin' on foot - or barefoot in your case.'

Alicia goes to speak but she cannot find the words. She feels weary and tired of trying to work out what she should do. She succumbs and chooses to take him up on his kind offer. All the while hoping he is not a psychotic serial killer. Will guides her off the bridge and starts walking across the meadow.

'We live in the house just over there', he says pointing in the direction of the farmhouse.

'Of course you do', Alicia mutters to herself slightly amused.

'Sorry what?', Will asks.

'Oh nothing. Sorry.'

As they approach the house, Alicia can smell the smoke from the chimney. She has never seen the building up close before, except when it was bits of rubble. It is an aesthetically pleasing home; a path leads up to a wooden front door with a handmade sign saying:

Welcome to Meadow View Cottage

The front of the house is full of organised clutter; a couple of spades, sweeping brush, a bike needing repair, and many items she could not identify. She had always referred to it as 'The Farmhouse' as it is surrounded by fields, but no working farm seems to be attached to it. A chicken coop was just about visible to the side of the house, along with a simple stable building. The warm glow from the windows of the cottage looks inviting but Alicia feels guilt crashing through her body as she thinks of Patrick somewhere out there.

'Look maybe I should come with you?', she says to Will.

Will shakes his head and looks up to the sky.

'Storm will be 'ere soon. It's best I go. I know these parts well', he says. 'No one ought to be out in it when it hits.'

Alicia swallows deeply.

Rolando and Ali have set up camp near the bridge. Ali, having returned home for provisions, sets up two deck chairs and pulls out a flask of tea from a rucksack. They sit down and take turns to sip from the mug.

'You could have bought two mugs you know', Rolando says.

'Oh shush! I was in a hurry', Ali responds. They sit watching the bridge.

'So no sign of Alicia whilst I was gone?, Ali asks.

'No nothing. I did see a deer though.'

Ali nods his head absentmindedly.

'How long are we going to stay here?', Ali asks.

'Well seeing is believing, and I want to see them come back through', Rolando says.

'Hmm. Lets hope we're right - that Patrick is with her. There was no sign of him when I went back up. Alicia's phone was on the side too', Ali says.

'And don't forget, his backpack was on the bridge', Rolando adds.

They sip their tea in silence.

'I mean, can you imagine, Ali? What if something magical has happened. It's about time. Dull as clouds around here. I bet they are having the time of their lives!'

'PATRICK!', Alicia yells at the top of her voice.

Will clutches his chest in shock.

'Blimey you got some lungs on ya', he says.

Patrick is still nowhere to be seen. A woman emerges from the door of the house wearing a dress and pinafore. She has short curly hair that frames her round face perfectly; her eyes glow with warmth; there is a gentleness to them.

'Goodness whatever is going on out here?', the woman asks.

'Quick summary - I don't know where she is from but her son is missin' somewhere round 'ere. And no, I don't know why she is wearin', Will pauses for a moment and looks towards Alicia's bare feet. 'Or rather, not wearin' any shoes.'

'Well now, fancy being out in that!', the woman says as she hurries next to Alicia placing her arm around her.

'I'm Gwen, Will's sister.'

'Now, Gwen', says Will. 'I'm gonna take the horse and have a gander for the boy. Best ya take Alicia inside eh?'

Gwen nods in agreement and ushers Alicia into the house. Alicia looks back towards Will who is heading towards the nearby stable.

'PATRICK!', Alicia yells.

Will and Gwen both jump this time.

'He'll find him don't you worry', Gwen says reassuringly as she too clutches her chest, her heart pounding slightly from Alicia's high-pitched scream.

'Has anyone ever told you you've got quite the lungs on you?'

As they enter the humble house Alicia is immediately struck by the overwhelming warmth that wraps itself around her body like a comforting hug. She has had little time to think about how cold she is but now that the warmth touches her skin she realises she is chilled to the bone. She begins to shiver. Gwen directs her to a chair by the fire and rushes to grab a knitted blanket to throw over her.

'Th-thank you', Alicia says.

'Just sit still for a moment. Get your bearings, lovey. I'll fetch us a nice cuppa', Gwen says.

Alicia wraps the blanket tightly round herself and begins to take in her surroundings. A small kitchen area adorns the far side of the room, with a rustic wooden table and mismatched wooden chairs placed around it. A large black stove dominates the far space, with metal pans hung up above it and some empty metal buckets discarded beside it. On the other side of the room stands a dark wooden dresser, with only one decorative item: a white vase with a simple pink flower painted on the front of it. The rest of the dresser's contents is full of plain looking plates, bowls and other practical items. A desk made from the same dark wood is in the corner, with books and newspapers piled high leaving little room to use it as an actual desk; an unlit lantern is precariously perched on the edge. Two large green fabric armchairs frame the log fire, one of which Alicia is currently sitting in. Above the fire hangs a watercolour painting of the stone bridge across the stream. She stares at the painting. It is beautifully simple.

'That bridge', Alicia says pointing towards the painting. 'What er… are your thoughts on it? The bridge I mean, not the painting. The painting is lovely obviously!'

Gwen walks over to her carrying two mugs of tea. She hands one to Alicia, and takes the other one with her to the opposite armchair. As Gwen sits down she stares up at the painting.

'What do I think of the bridge?', she says thoughtfully repeating Alicia's question.

'Er... yes. I mean, anything unusual about it?', Alicia emphasises.

Gwen stares at the image of the bridge for a minute. Alicia waits for her response; getting ever more hopeful of some profound meaningful insight with each passing second. *Yes she knows something,* Alicia thinks to herself as she observes Gwen studying the painting.

'Nope. Just a normal bridge', Gwen says finally. She laughs off the conversation. 'Drink your tea, dear'.

Alicia leans back in her chair and sips her tea, feeling deflated. Her eyes scan the room once more. No TV. No computer. No phone. Alicia's eyes widen. Her attention turns to her host who she observes is wearing a plain pinafore and simple check dress with thick stockings and slippers.

Gwen's eyes remain on the painting; she is staring at the signature in the bottom right corner:

Eric.

Her eyes glaze over as she reads this name over and over.

'Um I do have another question', Alicia says nervously.

Gwen straightens up in her seat realising she lost herself for a moment.

'What year is it?', Alicia asks.

Alicia assures herself that the thought running through her head is the stuff of fairytales and make believe, but she feels compelled to ask this simple question nonetheless. *Just to check,* she says to herself.

Gwen looks flabbergasted.

'Well I wasn't expecting that question!', she replies.

Alicia says nothing and waits patiently for the answer, causing Gwen to suddenly realise it is a genuine question.

'Oh right!', Gwen says feeling uncomfortable and shifting in her seat. 'Well it's the year it's been for the last 11 months. 1919.'

Gwen takes another sip of her tea, and casts a side eye at the door in the hope that Will will walk through it. Alicia reaches across to place her mug on the small table; her hand is trembling like a plane in turbulence as she tries to land the cup before it crashes to the floor. She looks over at the cluster of newspapers and leaps out of the chair.

'May I?', she asks Gwen pointing towards the papers.

'Oh, yes. Go head', she replies.

Gwen watches Alicia with concern as she rushes over to the desk and picks up one of the local newspapers. Alicia's eyes immediately find the date at the top.

'1,9 and 1,9', she whispers to herself. 'Uh oh.'

She turns back to Gwen.

'1919', Alicia says to her waving the paper up in the air manically.

Gwen stares at her blankly.

'This explains so much!', Alicia declares. 'And yet it explains so little!'

Alicia rubs her forehead. Gwen gets up from her chair and gestures with her arm for Alicia to return to her seat.

'Now come back and get warm by the fire. I think the cold has got to you—', Gwen says.

'Wait, what's this?', Alicia says unfolding the local newspaper.

She begins to read an item on the bottom of the front page.

'Wanted criminal', she reads. 'And he was spotted in this exact area!'

Gwen is suddenly looking very nervous; her eyes are wide, and she begins fidgeting with the bottom of her cardigan - wrapping it round her finger until it is so tight it feels numb. She looks towards the door and then looks back at Alicia.

'Oh now it is nothing, dear. Just a supposed criminal on the loose in these parts', Gwen says trying to sound reassuring.

Alicia looks at her open-mouthed.

'But my son is out there!', Alicia says.

'I don't think you need to worry', Gwen refutes.

'No need to worry!? MY SON IS—'

Will bursts through the door looking triumphant.

'Well look who I found!', he says.

Patrick sheepishly pokes his head through the doorway. 'Oh, hi mum', he says quietly upon spotting her.

Alicia runs over to Patrick and gives him a hug.

'Goodness you are cold', she says to him. 'What were you doing? What were you thinking?'

'I was just, you know, looking around. It was fun', he says. 'Did you know—'

Alicia interrupts quickly. 'Now-now Patrick let's remember we are guests to these complete strangers who have no idea what is going on', she says quietly.

'Why is your left eye twitching mum?'

Alicia shushes him. Gwen heads towards them and hands Patrick a hot drink. She encourages him to go and sit in front the fire.

'See, like I said. Safe 'n' sound', Will says happily.

Alicia watches all three of them drink their hot drinks and chat about the weather nonchalantly.

'Right. Well. Clearly I'm the mad one then', she says to herself raising her hands in the air.

'Well we really must be going now', Alicia talks a little louder to gain their attention. 'Thank you though. For finding him. For your hospitality.'

She proceeds to pick up her coat and starts to put it on but stops midway as she becomes aware that everyone is staring at her.

'What?', Alicia asks.

'I don't think you will be going anywhere', Will says sternly.

Will strides over to where Alicia is standing with a sombre look on his face. *He's coming for you,* her brain screams at her. She crosses her arms in front of her as if preparing for combat. Will reaches behind her, and tugs one of the curtains back. He either politely ignores her combative gesture, or is blissfully ignorant of it.

'Startin' to snow heavily now', he says.

Alicia looks outside and then looks down at her combat-ready arms. *You're a fool Alicia,* she thinks to herself as she quickly unfolds her arms and places them rigidly by her side. Completely exasperated by yet another obstacle to overcome she heads over to Patrick who is sitting in one of the armchairs, and flops down next to him.

'Fine', she says waving her hand in defeat.

Her head throbs. Her feet ache. She silently curses poohsticks. For a minute or so the only sound that can be heard is the loud slurps of drink that Patrick is taking. She spots the newspaper on the floor beside her which she dropped earlier.

'Oh I'm sorry', she says leaning forward to pick it up.

Gwen hurriedly scoops down and grabs it before Alicia has a chance to, and shoves it in one of the desk drawers. Gwen and Alicia exchange a look; one looks suspicious, the other looks bashful. Patrick observes this peculiar exchange.

'What was that paper?', he asks.

No one answers.

'Warm up there lad', Will says to Patrick. "I need to just go check on somethin.'

Will exits the room quickly. Gwen hurries behind him, glancing back at Alicia and Patrick with an attempt at a smile. As soon as Gwen is out of sight, Alicia jumps out of her seat and heads straight over to the desk drawer. She pulls out the now crumpled paper, and glances at the article once more.

'Mum, what is it?', Patrick asks in hushed tones.

'Nothing just stay there', she replies quietly.

Alicia continues to read:

If you see this man please let the local authorities know straightaway.

She is unable to make out much more of the details as the ink has smudged. She looks up from the paper and towards Patrick.

'As soon as the snow stops we leave here', she says.

Patrick extends his hands towards the fire and rubs them together. He looks over at Alicia quizzically. *He must have done something awful,* Alicia thinks to herself as she stares at the grainy sketch of the wanted man; he has a sharp, pointed nose and messy hair. His lips are thin and long like his face.

'Wait, what's that?', Patrick enquires as he jumps up and heads over to where she is standing.

He pulls the newspaper towards him and looks at the sketch. He squints and moves his face within a couple of inches of the image.

'I think I saw him', he says.

'What? Where?', Alicia says, startled by this revelation.

Will and Gwen re-enter the room talking in slightly raised tones. Alicia quickly stuffs the paper back into the drawer.

'But where is he!?', Will asks Gwen.

He lifts his hands in the air in exasperation. Both he and Gwen look flustered.

'Everything okay?', Alicia asks attempting to sound casual.

Gwen looks over at Alicia and shakes her head.

'Barnaby has gone. He is Will's', she hesitates, 'loyal companion. I was just telling him that he probably headed out after him to make sure he is okay.'

Gwen turns back to Will.

'I'm sure he *is* okay', Gwen says trying to sound comforting.

Will disappears into the next room again, grumbling as he goes. Gwen follows quickly behind.

'Mum, you must go and help look for him', Patrick says.

'What?', Alicia says in amazement.

'Will came and found me, and now you can do the same for him. Isn't that what you always say to me? We must treat others how we want to be treated?', he says.

Alicia gawps at Patrick.

'Well I admit I am fond of dogs but—', Alicia is interrupted by Gwen and Will.

'Right I need to go back out and look for Barnaby', Will announces to the room.

Gwen's face looks pained by this statement. She glances out at the falling snow with a look of grave concern.

'You can't leave him out there mum. He is all alone', Patrick says.

A tear rolls down his face. Alicia feels frozen to the spot. Everything about the last two days makes no sense to her. Her mind is flooded with visions and questions from the last 48 hours. She feels light-headed, almost giddy. She looks into Patrick's pleading eyes. A memory claws its way to the front of mind and pulls her in:

- - - -

Rhys's face looks out from the window of the car. He is trapped. He calls out to her but she cannot make out the words through the closed window. She runs towards him. The closer she gets the fainter his voice becomes.

- - - -

'Mum?', Patrick says.

Awoken from her past, she looks over at Will who is buttoning up his coat. Gwen is next to him clutching a hat that she is eager to give him. Will looks worried and noticeably paler than a few minutes ago. Alicia takes a deep breath in and straightens her posture.

'I will do it', Alicia declares.

Gwen and Will pause to look at her.

'Do what dear?', Gwen asks.

'Come with you, Will', Alicia says. 'And help.'

She looks over at Patrick and nods reassuringly.

Patrick wipes his eyes with the back of his hand and reveals a big grin on his face.

'Well I *think* I will anyway', Alicia says more hesitantly.

Patrick frowns.

'Nope I will. I will', Alicia says as she begins doing up her coat.

Gwen and Will look at each other.

'Er I think it is best ya stay here', Will says.

'Absolutely not. I have to repay you for your help', she says.

Will and Gwen look down at Alicia's bare feet.

'Ah', Alicia says. 'Do you happen to have any shoes?'

Will shrugs at Gwen who looks at him with apprehension.

'Time is pressin'. I'll just get her some of those wellies in the back', he says to Gwen.

Will is reluctant but nevertheless he hurries off to acquire the wellies, keen to get on his way and not engage in a debate.

'And maybe one of the coats hanging up too', Gwen calls out after him, as she surveys Alicia's thin raincoat.

As they wait for Will, silence fills the room; the awkwardness is palpable.

'I had a dog once. Many years ago', Alicia tells Gwen in some attempt to break the silent deadlock.

'They do find a special place in your heart, don't they?', she continues.

Gwen stares, unsure what to say.

'Um yes. I guess so, dear', she replies.

'Ah yes, their waggy tails - always happy to see you', Alicia says.

'Um… Will, have you found the wellies and coat yet?', Gwen calls out.

Gwen looks back at Alicia with a sheepish smile. She begins twirling the bottom of her cardigan around her finger again.

'I'm sorry. I am not helping am I? Talking about the joy of dogs when Barnaby is missing', Alicia says. 'So what is Barnaby like?'

'Barnaby? Well, he is... like family to us you see', Gwen replies somewhat cautiously.

'I understand completely', Alicia says with confidence. 'I bet he gives you a good licking too.'

Alicia chuckles to herself and looks over at Patrick. He stares at her and shakes his head as if to say *what are you doing.*

'Pardon?', Gwen says.

'Well it's what they do isn't it', says Alicia. Her tone less confident now as she detects an air of annoyance in Gwen's demeanour.

'They? What do you mean by that?', Gwen says looking a little more animated. 'I can assure you Barnaby has never licked me in his life! He is a good man. And, and a good... friend to Will.'

Alicia stares. Her face begins to flush a bright shade of red.

'Man?', Alicia says. 'Oh.'

Gwen and Alicia stare at one another. *Right, so not a dog,* Alicia thinks. *Noted.*

CHAPTER 5
THE COMPANIONS

"Only those who will risk going too far can possibly find out how far one can go". - T. S. Eliot

The howl of the wind echoes through the trees as if the woodland is screaming out in pain. The clouds' quest to rid themselves of their load creates an unrelenting blizzard of snow. Large white snowflakes assault the faces of Will and Alicia as they try to push their way through the storm. Every step they take requires more effort than the last; the snow on the ground becomes ever more stubborn, refusing to relinquish its grip on their boots.

'Bar—', Will chokes on the incoming snow. 'Barnaby', he shouts.

It's all a dream, Alicia tells herself; these words have become a mantra banging in her head like a beating drum. The thought of waking up in her familiar bed, safe at home, keeps her spirit warm during this battle against the winter beast. *How is it even winter here anyway,* she thinks. Another layer of confusion had been added to her already bulging brain; it was July back home, yet November here. She tries to look around in earnest for Barnaby but all she sees is flurries of white flashes in front of her eyes. She has no idea where they are, nor what direction the farmhouse is in. Her trust is completely put in Will, who reassures her that he knows his way around even in a blizzard.

Alicia hears a loud rumble and feels a sharp thud on her shoulder which nearly throws her off balance. It sends a surging pain down through her arm. She frantically looks behind her, thinking she is under attack. Every pulse point vibrates as her heart furiously pumps blood around her body. She screams. Will turns to her quickly and brushes a large chunk of snow from her shoulder.

'It's okay - just some snow fallin' from the tree branch above', he tells her.

Alicia nods and tries to bring her breathing under control. She looks up for signs of any more trees shaking off their unwanted baggage. Will tugs on her coat and gestures for her to follow him. Although focussed on their task of finding Barnaby, she cannot help but feel queasy at the thought of a criminal lurking somewhere; a thought that refuses to leave her. She imagines menacing eyes watching them, giving her more chills than the snow does. *What fool would possibly be out in this weather*, she rationalises with herself. Then, realising the irony of that thought, she looks behind her - *just to check*.

Visibility remains poor and shows little sign of improving any time soon. Alicia begins to wonder if they will get trapped, or worse, buried out here if the snow does not ease. Her feet slip back-and- forth inside the borrowed wellies. So far the snow has successfully stayed out of the boots but as it deepens it threatens to invade her dry feet's sanctuary. Alicia begins to doubt her logic for being out here with a perfect stranger seeking another stranger, and leaving her boy with a stranger. She tries to push her panic back down, and keep it locked away. There is little chance to get to know Will in this circumstance, except to acknowledge that he has remarkable body strength to push himself and her through this storm. He has already pulled her from the clutches of the snow several times when her own body strength failed her.

'It's like finding a needle in a haystack', Alicia shouts to Will over the sound of the wind.

Will looks a little pained by this comment for a second, causing Alicia to regret the abruptness of her tone.

'I know we'll find him', he refutes.

Alicia hears what sounds like branches breaking somewhere in the distance. She jerks her head around trying to check for signs of life.

'I've never seen snow like this round here', she says. Will glances at her out of the corner of his eye.

'Except for the last year. And the year before that. And —'

'Oh yes. Of course. Except for that', Alicia interrupts, realising her lack of knowledge of early 1900s weather.

Alicia's boundaries are being pushed to the limit; her hair is no longer neatly tied back, her clothes are no longer clean, her nails are becoming chipped and broken. She feels out of control, completely thrust from the safety of her routine. Throughout this whole ordeal she has battled to keep a lid on her growing agitation. She longs to be back cleaning her kitchen, folding laundry, writing shopping lists: all of these things are like her comfort blanket. So long as she sticks to routine, she always felt nothing bad or unexpected could happen. At least, that is how she chose to approach her life since Rhys lost his.

'H-help.'

'Wait a minute', she says clutching Will's arm. 'Do you hear something?'

They both remain still, straining to make out a sound that is neither the howling wind nor their heavy breaths. The sound of a faint cry comes and goes with the wind.

'H-help.'

'Yes!', says Will. 'I hear it!'

Gwen and Patrick are sat by the fire, each with a blanket wrapped around them. Every so often they glance outside at the snow, and both feel a shard of worry pierce their stomach.

'So are they married?', Patrick asks Gwen.

'Who?', she replies.

'Will and Barnaby', Patrick says.

Gwen looks alarmed.

'What?', Patrick asks.

'No of course they're not. How could they be?', she replies, shocked by his casual tone.

'Well Ali and Rolando have been for years. And my—', Patrick looks downcast. 'My mum and dad were. Loads of people are.'

'Well yes, I know marriage is common. But—', The fire begins to dim.

'Oh dear I mustn't let that go out', Gwen says leaping into action.

Patrick studies Gwen as she throws some more logs onto the fire, and prods it with a metal tong. He is intrigued by her edgy, slightly nervous manner.

'There we are', she says watching the fire come back to life.

Gwen returns to her seat. She reaches down beside her.

'Well now, I think we need to take our mind off things. What about a game?', she says holding up a battered looking pack of cards.

Patrick nods.

'Do you have an Xbox 360?', he asks.

He looks around the room and is surprised to find no signs of any electronics. Gwen looks at him, still holding the cards up in the air.

'A Box of what?', she asks. 'These are your standard 52 box of cards.'

Gwen looks at Patrick. Patrick looks back at Gwen.

'Ohh-kay', he says with an eye roll. 'Where's your TV?'

'Tea?', asks Gwen.

They continue to stare at each other, both equally unsure what they should say next.

'Over there!', Alicia shouts.

She points towards an opening in the trees where she can just about make out a figure moving on the ground. Will and Alicia stumble over the mounting snow as they head towards the blurry figure. They clutch each others' arms to steady themselves.

'H-e-l-p', comes the cry of a man's voice again.

'Barnaby?', calls Will.

The figure gradually comes into focus as they draw near; a man is laying on his back half covered in snow, and waving his arms around in a desperate attempt to be seen.

'Oh th-thank g-goodness. You f-found me!', the man stutters through shivers. 'Every t-time I try to w-walk I lose my f- footing. I think I have b-badly hurt my ankle.'

'Quick, help me get him up', Will instructs Alicia. 'If we each take an arm we should be able to manage.'

Alicia stumbles again as she makes her way to Barnaby's side by half-crawling and half-walking.

'I-I', she spits out some snow. 'I'm Alicia', she says to Barnaby.

Barnaby wipes away the snow from his face and looks up at her. She looks down at him, and for a moment she's caught in a trance wondering why he looks so familiar.

'Well who-whoever you are', Barnaby says. 'I'm b-bloomin' glad you're here! Th-thank you.'

Alicia leaps to her feet and takes a step away from him.

'You - you're the man. The man in the paper. The wanted criminal!', she cries.

Will is already crouched down ready to lift up Barnaby from the floor. He shakes his head in exasperation.

'Barnaby won't hurt ya', Will says.

'So you're harbouring a criminal?', Alicia says turning to Will.

'Only in the eyes of the law!', he retaliates.

Alicia scrunches her face up as she tries to make sense of this counter argument.

'Look we have no time for this. Let's get him up and try to get back to the house', Will says desperately.

He tries to lift Barnaby on his own but fails. Alicia feels unsure what to do but the snow is coming down fast, and she is as lost without them as they are without her. She heads over to Barnaby and crouches down next to him, pulling his arm up over his shoulder. Will mouths the words *thank you* to her, and they both lift him up. Barnaby groans in pain, Will and Alicia groan from the strain. Barnaby's face wrinkles in pain as his ankle gets knocked about in the snow.

'I c-can't p-put any weight on it', Barnaby cries.

Will and Alicia begin to move forward slowly, carrying the full weight of Barnaby who does his best to hop along without falling over and dragging them all down with him. A couple of times they all end up flat out in the snow.

'Ahhhh', they cry collectively as they land face first again in a powdery mound of snow in perfect synchronicity.

'I assume you know where you're going Will?, Alicia asks breathlessly as they all try to pull each other up off the ground.

'Yes', came his short response. He had little breath to spare.

Alicia's mind was racing. Here she was in the middle of a snowstorm in 1919 with a criminal half hanging off her. She looks over at Will.

'Can you promise me my son is not in any danger? I mean we are not letting—'

She pauses and lowers her voice to a loud whisper.

'We're not letting a mass murderer loose in the house with my son are we?'

Barnaby looks at her.

'I mean, I can hear you', Barnaby says. 'And I'm not a murderer.'

After a while all three are leaning on each other for support. Exhausted, cold and disoriented from the snow no-one has spoken a word for a long time. Logic seemed a thing of the past; Alicia begins to wonder if she was always in 1919 and whether her life with Rhys was all a lie. Then she begins to wonder if this was all some elaborate hoax, and a TV crew will appear at any moment with a large cash reward for making a fool of herself.

'W-Will!', she cries feebly. 'L-look there's light.'

Alicia spots the faintest flicker of a light in the distance. Will nods with a smile.

'Yep. That'd be the house.'

Alicia looks at Will in awe. *He actually did it,* she thought. Will got them back to the house as he promised.

They burst through the farmhouse door bringing with them flurries of snow flakes, and a waft of icy cold air. Gwen and Patrick jump to their feet in alarm at the sudden dramatic entrance. Patrick had been trying to explain to Gwen what an Xbox 360 is; Gwen is relieved to see them, and seems grateful for the interruption to the conversation. She throws open her arms to all three of them, a broad smile lights up her face.

'Oh thank goodness you are back safely', Gwen says with much delight.

She touches Alicia on the arm, leans towards her and whispers:

'Your boy has a vivid imagination by the way.'

Alicia looks over at Patrick, who just shrugs and smiles at her. Alicia smiles back.

'Well done', Patrick says to her. His dimples begin to emerge as his smile grows.

Alicia feels warmth creep up through her body; it was either the warmth of the fire reaching her, or the fact that her son no longer thinks she is a bore. Gwen helps Will take Barnaby through to one of the back rooms, keen to attend to his wounded ankle. Alicia removes the boots and her coat, and slumps down in one of the armchairs. She lets out a big sigh; her whole body aches as the adrenaline begins to leave it. Patrick perches on the arm next to her.

'You did it', he says.

'Yes. Yes I suppose I did something. Like release a potential murderer into the back room', she says quietly.

'What?, asks Patrick.

'Oh never you mind', she says pulling him into a hug.

Alicia wakes to the sound of clattering pans and the murmur of chatter. She looks around the room waiting for her eyes to focus, and wipes away some dribble from the edge of her mouth. Her body feels stiff as she pulls herself up from the armchair. She sees Gwen and Patrick busy in the kitchen, Will is hunched over looking out of the window, and Barnaby is sat in one of the mismatched dining chairs examining the side of his ankle.

'Oh hello, you've rejoined the land of the conscious again', Gwen says chuckling as she places some bowls of soup on the table. 'Just in time too', she adds, pointing towards the soup and a vacant chair.

Alicia smiles and slowly heads over to the table to take her seat. Patrick is already tucking into some soup with much enthusiasm. Barnaby observes him for a second and smiles.

'Snow has stopped', announces Will as he heads over to the last vacant seat.

'Hungry lad', Barnaby says to Alicia, gesturing towards Patrick.

She shifts uneasily in her chair, remembering how little she knows about him. Or indeed how little she knows anyone here. She manages a half smile, recognising this was his attempt to break the ice. Only now was she able to fully take in what Barnaby looks like, beyond his anguished face out in the snow earlier. His hair looks like it has a life of its own, sticking up in all different directions. A single scar is faintly visible by his left ear. He is lean and tall, but stoops as if trying to bring himself down to everyone else's height. She glances down at his hands and has to do a double-take; she counts 8 fingers in total. Barnaby spots her surprised look.

'Don't worry', he says. 'You're not the only one who has to count my fingers twice. Souvenir of the war.'

Alicia nods sympathetically.

'I didn't mean to stare', she responds.

'I know you have questions', Barnaby continues, choosing to change topic.

He picks up a spoon and shovels some soup into his mouth. Alicia dips her spoon in her soup but does not take a sip. She looks around the table; everyone is focussed on their food. She turns back to Barnaby.

'Well I'm not sure this is the place', she says nodding towards Patrick.

'All you need to know is that I have done no harm and will do no harm', Barnaby says to Alicia with a smile.

There is a sudden chink of porcelain as Patrick proudly places his spoon in his empty bowl.

'Why would you do harm anyway?', Patrick asks Barnaby. 'And why would you think that?', he asks Alicia.

Gwen begins collecting up the empty soup bowls, feeling a great sense of contentment at the sight of the empty soup bowls; all except for Alicia's.

'At least have a little bit', Gwen says to Alicia looking disappointed. 'It'll do you good.'

Alicia nods and dutifully begins scooping up some soup. Patrick taps his fingers on the table to signify he is still waiting for some answers. Alicia frowns at him. He stops tapping. Barnaby looks over at him and they exchange a chuckle. Barnaby turns back to Alicia and says:

'Given you thought I was a murderer—'

Patrick gasps.

'I'm assuming you never read the full article in the local rag?', he continues.

Alicia shakes her head as she scoops up some more soup. Suddenly her stomach is crying out for more food; she cannot remember the last time she ate something. Everything else pales into insignificance compared to the warm sustenance the soup brings. She nods along out of sync with what Barnaby is saying.

'The reason I'm wanted by the law is because a letter I had written to Will was intercepted. It was, um... just talking about our future together.'

Barnaby pauses waiting for a response. Alicia keeps nodding. Patrick stares at him waiting for the next instalment of the story. Gwen shoots Barnaby an encouraging look, urging him to continue.

'So obviously it is rather frowned upon to plan a future with.... a man. Illegal in fact', Barnaby says, feeling less sure of himself as he tries to gauge Alicia's reaction.

Alicia places the spoon in her empty bowl and rubs her stomach feeling immense satisfaction. She smiles and looks towards Barnaby.

'Yes, so you wrote a letter planning your future', she stops speaking abruptly.

Alicia looks at Will and then at Barnaby.

'Oh I see', she says.

Her brain begins to recharge thanks to the fuel of the food, and gives her a further nudge. *It's 1919 of course,* she thinks.

'Ohhh I really do see', she says.

'I have no idea what is happening', says Patrick.

Barnaby continues, feeling buoyant now that he can see Alicia is unfazed.

'Fortunately the letter did not have Will's full details on it - full name and address. The letter was obtained by my old landlady before I even had time to send it. She always had it in for me mind', he says. 'Unfortunately she is quite well connected, hence local rags running stories on me.'

Barnaby folds his arms tightly across his chest; his body becomes tense. He looks over at the desk where one of the newspapers is sat, and feels queasy at the thought of the article written about him.

'She went snooping', Gwen adds. 'She was on a mission to find something on you. All because you showed her no interest.'

Will pats Gwen on the arm, both to comfort her and to dissuade her from getting herself riled up about it again. It did not seem to be working.

'And another thing', Gwen continues, 'you did so much for that landlady. Helped fix up her house, sort her garden out. People just take advantage of your generous soul.'

Barnaby blushes. He feels underserving of such a compliment, but he is grateful for Gwen's loyalty and gives her a warm smile in appreciation.

'We just want to be happy. Live a simple life in the country. Recover from the war', Barnaby says, turning back towards Alicia.

'Like what everyone wants; to live their short life in a meaningful way', Will adds.

Barnaby stares out of the window to distract himself, sensing his composure is about to slip.

'War?', Patrick mouths to Alicia.

Before she can respond, Patrick spots a tin model of a train in the far corner of the room. Distracted by this discovery, he jumps off his chair and eagerly goes to inspect the object.

'Oh, and by the way ', Barnaby says. 'I don't go round licking people.'

A cheeky smile spreads across his face. Alicia turns a little red and looks down at her empty bowl.

'Ah so you heard about that little mix up', Alicia says looking at Gwen.

'I don't understand why a person would lick another person anyway', Patrick calls out from across the corner of the room.

Everyone else stops and stares at one another with suppressed smiles. Patrick walks slowly back to join them all at the dining table, rubbing his chin. He looks quizzically at Barnaby.

'So you wrote a letter to him', Patrick says pointing to Will. 'And that is illegal?'

Patrick looks up at the ceiling, as if waiting for the answer to drop into his head.

'Nope. I don't understand', he concludes.

'Ah yes, Patrick now about that', Alicia says. 'The thing is', she leans in towards him and whispers, 'it would appear this is the year 1919. A man, well, choosing to make plans with a man is illegal.'

Patrick jumps to his feet and slams his hand down on the table.

'Wait! You mean we travelled back?', he squeals with delight.

Gwen, Will and Barnaby all stop what they are doing and stare at Patrick. Their faces full of curiosity and unease.

'Do you think we will get back. No actually, go back-forward okay?', Patrick asks Alicia.

'I hope so', she replies clasping her hands together as if in silent prayer. 'I still don't know if this is all a dream to be honest.'

Patrick suddenly jumps in front of Alicia and growls loudly.

'Ahhh! What was that?', Alicia cries.

'I read somewhere you can wake yourself from a dream by being frightened', he says. 'I don't think this is a dream.'

'Yes, well thank you for that Patrick but I think I have had ample frights already', she replies.

Alicia realises her hosts are clueless what she and Patrick are talking about. She turns to find them gawping at her. She waves a hand dismissively in front of her face and laughs.

'Just an inside joke we have', she says, trying to sound convincing.

The three hosts laugh nervously, clearly none-the-wiser. Patrick turns towards Barnaby and Will, and takes a moment to allow the right words to form in his mind before he speaks them out loud. He taps his chin and brings his eyebrows together, striking a philosophical pose.

'I think one day you won't have to hide yourself', Patrick says thoughtfully.

Alicia gives a gentle nod of encouragement to Patrick, and a rather awkward smile towards Will and Barnaby as she spots the bemusement on their faces.

'That was well said, Patrick', Alicia whispers to Patrick.

Alicia turns back towards Will and Barnaby.

'What may be the case now, will not be in the future', she says.

There is a brief moment of silence.

'I understand', says Will.

He does not understand. Will and Barnaby exchange a puzzled look with each other. They both find their guests peculiar and entertaining. Alicia senses this.

'Well, lets just put it like this. To us, there is no crime here - only love', she says softly. Will and Barnaby are taken aback.

'I've never known kindness like this from a stranger', Will says. 'Not 'bout this situation anyway. 'Scuse me'.

Will promptly leaves the room. Barnaby turns to Alicia and smiles, placing his three-fingered hand next to her hand.

'You'd never think it, but he is the emotional one', he says.

'Just wait, he'll be back in a minute saying he had to check on something, but he's probably crying his eyes out in the other room', Gwen adds.

Alicia was surprised by this revelation. Will returns to the room, red-faced and puffy-eyed.

'Sorry 'bout that. Just had to check on the windows', Will says.

'Your excuses are getting more far-fetched', Gwen says under her breath with a smile.

The night owl can be heard calling out in the distance beyond the walls of the cottage where everyone now sleeps, except for Alicia and Gwen. Patrick is curled up on a chair near the fire which crackles gently in the background. Alicia quietly gets up from the other armchair and goes to join Gwen, who is sat at the kitchen table looking thoughtfully at the wall.

'Oh couldn't you sleep, dear?', she asks Alicia as she sits down opposite her.

Alicia shakes her head.

'This usually does the trick', Gwen says.

She stands up and pours some hot cocoa from the stove into a mug, and hands it to Alicia.

'But this does the trick more', she continues.

Gwen grabs a bottle of whisky and adds a big slug into each of their drinks.

'My mother's remedy', she says with a smile.

'A remedy for the child or for the mother?', Alicia asks.

They both let out a little silent laugh. It felt good to laugh, even for a second.

'I never asked whereabouts you are from? Not from these parts I assume?', Gwen asks.

'Oh - here and there. I mean, we do know these parts well. But it has changed a lot.'

'How long has it been since you were last here?'

'Oh... feels like a hundred years!', Alicia says with half a smile as she takes a big sip of cocoa.

Gwen glances at Alicia's wedding ring.

'What does you husband do?'

Alicia grips the warm mug tightly.

'He died.'

'Oh I'm sorry, dear. The war has taken so many', Gwen says sadly. 'I assume it was the war?'

'So, what about you?', Alicia asks, wishing to change the subject.

'Oh', Gwen swallows deeply and shakes her head dismissively. 'Well...'. Gwen's voice trails off.

Alicia can see the pain wash over Gwen's face as she relives some poignant memories; something Alicia knows all too well.

'He disappeared', Gwen continues. 'The only man I ever really loved. Twenty-two years old and suddenly he never came back. I never saw or heard from him again. No-one has ever managed to trace him.'

Gwen moves her mug in gentle circles trying to mix the whisky and cocoa further; she stares into the contents trying to distract herself from her feelings.

'That's terrible', Alicia says.

Gwen nods but keeps her eyes fixed on her drink. Alicia wishes she could say something that would bring comfort but words escape her. She reaches out and places her hand gently on Gwen's arm, just for a second or two.

'He was born just up the road at Privy Farm. We grew up together from a young age. Neither of us really knew anywhere but here. Didn't matter though; it was enough for us. We were engaged by the time we were 21', Gwen recalls.

'What was his name?', Alicia asks.

'Eric', Gwen replies. 'To be honest I never really knew what it was to feel lonely until he left. And—'.

Gwen stops to regain some control as her voice breaks with emotion.

'He never knew I was pregnant either. Never had chance to tell him. It would have caused a huge scandal but we both knew we were going to marry soon anyway. Well, fate obviously had different plans because not long after he left me, so did my baby. And now here I am.'

Gwen shrugs her shoulders in attempt to shake off her feelings but it is no good. She places her mug back down and buries her face in her hands.

'I'm sorry', she says through her hands. 'I don't know why I'm telling you all this.'

'No I'm sorry. So sorry. How awful for you', Alicia says reassuringly.

The two women sit in silence but this time the silence feels easy not awkward; united in their shared experience of grief.

'If only we could go back in time', Gwen says finally.

Alicia almost drops her cup, spilling some of the contents over the table.

'Oh! Don't worry, dear', Gwen says as she jumps up and grabs a nearby cloth. 'Whisky is setting in now I suspect.'

After Gwen has finished cleaning up the pool of cocoa, she turns to Alicia and finishes her earlier thought.

'It'd just be nice to rewrite some mistakes. Choose different paths. Make new choices', she says.

Alicia nods, suddenly wondering if she should be doing something more profound during her time in 1919. Wondering what future she would return to if she changed the past. These thoughts were too much for her weary head, and so she chooses to file them away for now. Instead she pulls out another thought that has been lurking in the back of her mind since earlier.

'What will happen, you know, with Will and Barnaby?', Alicia asks.

Gwen breathes in deeply through gritted teeth. It is a question she dreads to hear.

'I suspect they will both go somewhere different. Somewhere Barnaby is less likely to be recognised' Gwen replies through muted tears.

'Oh no I didn't mean to upset you', Alicia says softly.

'Oh it's okay', Gwen says wiping away a tear with a hanky she pulls out from her sleeve. 'It will just feel so lonely to be here without them. To be honest it's those lot who write for the local rag. It's like a witch-hunt - just 'coz someone local spotted him.'

Alicia wonders what Gwen would make of the world she has come from. So much has changed. She thought of Rolando and Ali and the life they are living.

'Could you go with them?', Alicia asks. Gwen shakes her head.

'We talked about it. But it'd be tough with the work they will be doing. Moving about quite a bit', Gwen replies.

'Besides this has been my home for so long now, it would be hard to leave it', Gwen says, looking nostalgically around the room.

'To be honest, I just hope the world learns from the war. What is important and what isn't', Gwen says. 'Surely we will never see another war like this one ever again. It would be madness.'

Alicia places her cup back down, unable to finish the last drops. She glances around the room, taking in the simplicity of their living.

'He painted that by the way', Gwen says gesturing towards the painting of the bridge above the fireplace. 'Eric. He was very creative. Carved some beautiful woodwork. He could even make a stick beautiful.'

'A stick?', Alicia's posture straightens. 'Um... he liked sticks did he? Any in particular?'

Alicia knew this was a ridiculous question but she felt compelled to ask it because of the ridiculous situation she found herself in.

'Er.... I mean he did whittle', Gwen says trying to find some logic to the question. 'Well yes, I suppose you could say he liked sticks, he spent many hours whittling them.'

Alicia felt her mind brim with whimsical thoughts. A vanishing man whittling a magic stick is the closest she has come to any explanation. Alicia shakes her head and laughs at herself.

'Actually', Gwen says thoughtfully. 'I do recall he was working on something before he disappeared.'

Gwen pinches her forehead with her fingers, trying to prize out the memory. Alicia leans in eagerly, ready for the next instalment.

'It was perhaps a couple of days before he vanished. He was quite upset, distraught almost, that the local farmer was going to cut down a tree', Gwen says, pausing to allow time for the memory to fully form.

'Ah yes I remember now. It was a Rowan tree. Or fid na ndruad he called it once', Gwen says.

Alicia looks at Gwen puzzled.

'It means Wizard's Tree. I think', Gwen continues. 'It was one of our last conversations come to think of it.'

Gwen half smiles and wipes away a tear; she feels a cocktail of emotions stirring inside her.

'Gosh I haven't thought about that since he went missing. Never seemed important. But odd nonetheless how much it affected him', Gwen reflects.

Alicia takes a moment to ponder this new information. *Did it mean anything?,* she thought. Not sure what to make of this story, Alicia gently squeezes Gwen's arm with her hand before returning to the comfort of the armchair and warm fire.

CHAPTER 6
HOMETIME

"The journey is my home". - Muriel Rukeyser

The morning sun emerges triumphantly with no clouds to block its delightful rays of light. Birdsong fills the air as they flutter through the trees and shrubbery, seeking sustenance beneath the snow. Will walks out of the front door, closely followed by Alicia.

'Are ya sure ya want to head out?', he asks her. 'The snow is still thick on the ground. And ya footwear is... well... odd for this weather.'

He looks down at the old slip-on shoes Gwen has given her. They pinch the sides of Alicia's toes as she walks.

'Oh yes! We must go. Thank you so much for your generosity', Alicia says.

Patrick walks out of the front door in a coat much too big for him. His hands are unable to make it to the end of the sleeves. He looks down at the snow.

'I've never seen so much snow here before', he says excitedly.

Gwen and Barnaby emerge and stand in the doorway, peering out at the white-covered landscape against the backdrop of the vivid blue sky.

'Nice to look at rather than be in', Barnaby remarks. 'You sure you don't want to wait until it eases? Will could lead you on horseback to...?'

Barnaby waits hoping that Alicia will add in the place she is going. As tempting as it is for Alicia to reply with, *under the bridge to about 100 years into the future,* she thought better of it.

'Oh no it's fine, believe it or not we know the route home from here very well', Alicia assures everyone.

No one feels reassured. Including Alicia.

'Do please take care of yourselves', Gwen instructs her.

Gwen looks down at Alicia's footwear.

'Are you sure you don't want to take my wellies?', she asks.

Alicia shakes her head, already feeling they have taken advantage of their hospitality. She hesitates to give Gwen a hug but Gwen shows no such hesitation. She pulls her into a tight embrace. Alicia feels a sudden rush of fondness for Gwen. Patrick flaps the oversized coat sleeves at everyone in an attempt to wave goodbye.

Their concerned hosts watch them walk away for longer than Alicia would have liked.

'Whatever you do don't fall over', she says to Patrick. 'Or else they will whizz us back to the safety of their house before you can say— ahhhhh!'

Alicia stumbles in the snow.

'Only messing', she calls back to Gwen, Will and Barnaby.

A forced smile creeps across her face.

'I don't think you were messing', Patrick says.

Patrick's head peeps out through the top of the oversized coat which drapes itself unflatteringly over his body; from afar he resembles an oversized bowling pin. He wobbles unsteadily as he slips and slides in the untouched snow. Alicia is immersed in her own snowy battle; she flinches from the tight fitting shoes that do little to shield her feet from the cold. The nurturing warmth of the farmhouse now feels like a distant memory.

'How much longer?', Patrick mumbles.

'A little longer. We've only been going for two minutes!'

Patrick grumbles incoherently. *Next time*, he tells himself, *I will bring a sledge.* Busy making a mental list in his head of all the items he will need with him, he suddenly becomes aware of an irritating ache coming from the waist of his trousers. He pauses and unbuttons the coat, fumbling around the waist to find the source of discomfort.

'Aha!', he exclaims. 'I totally forget about this.'

Alicia turns around and sees Patrick waving the velvety-grey stick in the air.

'Where on earth have you been hiding that', she says nervously glancing at his pocketless clothing.

Patrick pinches the elastic of the trouser waist.

'I just stuffed it here. Not the whole time, just didn't want to forget it when we left.'

'But how could you not notice it.... And why *that* stick?', Alicia asks.

'I dunno', he said. 'I kinda like it. Found it in my backpack and threw it in the water to test whether it vanished, and then it just turned up on—'

'The grass - well snow?', Alicia interrupts

Patrick looks surprised. Alicia's mind feels ready to burst from all the questions it brims with, and all of the seemingly bizarre answers it is conjuring.

Alicia takes the stick from him and begins studying it. She runs her fingers softly down the side, it feels smooth with a slight peach-fuzz. How weird that they both seem drawn to a random stick, she muses.

'You think it's magic don't you', Patrick says with a smirk and an air of satisfaction.

He felt a great sense of enjoyment watching his play-by-the-book mother contemplate something as extraordinary as a magical stick. Alicia glances up at him with one eyebrow slightly raised.

'The whole thing is ludicrous', she declares.

Patrick lets out a disappointed sigh. She hands the stick back to him and they continue their treacherous walk through the snowy meadow.

'Well things like this are always happening', Patrick says.

'Yes but you are talking about on TV and films aren't you?', Alicia says.

'Well.... yeah', Patrick says unperturbed.

'Life isn't like a film though.'

'Well at the moment it is', he responds.

Alicia can tell they are not going to get anywhere with this conversation.

'What do you think is happening then?', he asks, not wishing to end the topic.

Alicia thinks for a moment.

'Honestly? I think and hope this is all some vivid dream.'

'Good luck with that', says Patrick through a snigger.

Alicia shoots him a look, although why she feels annoyed at him she does not know. After another minute she responds.

'Sorry Patrick. I'm just feeling frustrated and tired by this whole thing'.

'Time travel is meant to be fun though', he quips.

Alicia does not respond to this, instead she thinks about how much the shoes are hurting her. How much her body aches. How much she wants tea and a chocolate biscuit, and to watch her favourite TV show - to be a spectator and see someone else go through escapades from the comfort of her sofa.

***

'The bridge!', they say together pointing at the stony arch coming into focus.

Its grey architecture stands defiantly amongst the sea of white. Patrick begins to pick up speed and overtakes Alicia, who urges him to take it steady. He disregards her plea with a dismissive wave of his handless coat sleeve. He almost breaks into a run but the combination of the long coat and deep snow prevent his legs from freely moving. All of a sudden he finds himself colliding with the ground.

'Patrick!', Alicia calls out.

Landing on his belly, gravity and the slippery snow work together to pull him down the incline and deposit him ungracefully into the stream. The icy shell smashes under his weight to reveal the water below that now splashes all over his face thanks to its new found freedom. Patrick remains still for a second trying to work out what just happened to him. Suddenly a hand firmly grips his arm, and he is pulled up from the cold water. Alicia groans, he feels twice as heavy thanks to his water-logged coat.

'I did say be careful', Alicia says, trying to squeeze some of the water out of his jacket. Patrick remains unusually quiet; feeling too cold, wet and uncomfortable to speak.

'Right l-lets w-work out how to ge-get out of here before we both fr—fr—freeze t-to death', she says, her teeth now chattering as the consequence of standing in ice cold water takes hold of her body.

She turns and looks towards the bridge, observing the crisp layer of ice that rests on top of the usually vibrant stream. *How will we get under the bridge*, Alicia mulls to herself as she studies the icing on the water. Lifting up her right leg, and using Patrick for balance, she attempts to break through some of the ice with the heel of her shoe. It works.

'It's o-only a th-thin layer of ice. I-I think we can b-break our w-way through', she says.

Alicia grabs Patrick's damp coat sleeve and begins heading towards the bridge; carefully breaking the ice with each step. She groans in discomfort, unsure how much longer her feet will cope. Patrick trundles behind her, his head hung in misery. As they reach the underpass of the bridge they proceed towards the centre. Alicia inhales deeply and smacks her heel against the final section of ice.

'Ouch!', she cries.

Alicia stares at the free-flowing water for a few seconds. Gesturing for Patrick to stay still, they pause and watch the water.

'It's n-not still', she says, shivering more violently now. 'Not l-like b-before - it w-was f-frozen in time like a-a ..... picture.'

She turns towards Patrick.

'Usually the w-water is d-deadly still - s-surely m-must be linked to w-what is happening to us? The w-water d-does n-not usually act like th-that.'

Patrick holds out a shaking hand, in it he clutches the stick.

'M-m-maybe it on-only w-w-w-works if—', he shivers uncontrollably.

He accidentally drops the stick; they watch it submerge into the water, and gasp as all of a sudden the water becomes still. A small circle of water is frozen with no ice. They look at each other and then look back down at the still water.

'Is i-it m-me or is e-everything s-spinning', Alicia says looking back towards Patrick whose eyes are wide with alarm.

'Ahhh', they scream.

As if some invisible force had pushed them over, they find them themselves falling backwards in opposite directions from one another. Alicia clings to Patrick's coat sleeve for as long as possible before she collides with the rocky floor of the stream. She spits water from her mouth and pushes her body up with her hands, her bottom is drenched and stings from taking the brunt of the fall. She blindly reaches behind her, her eyes foggy from water, and pulls on the sleeve of Patrick's coat.

'C-come on lets g-get out of the w-water'.

She heads out from underneath the bridge, starting to feel feverish from the cold and wet.

'Oh my—', she exclaims.

The air feels noticeably warmer as if someone has just turned the heating on. Her frozen nose feels instant relief. She stands for moment and allows the change in temperature to encase her body.

'Alicia!'

She instantly recognises the voice. Alicia looks around, she can make out a figure moving closer to her across the grass; it is Rolando. He hurries towards the edge of the bank and eagerly holds out his hand for her to grab on to. Another figure appears several feet behind him. Alicia moves towards Rolando, and he pulls her up.

The second figure comes into view; Ali appears next to Alicia with a half eaten biscuit in one hand. He decides to throw the remainder of the biscuit into the stream having suddenly lost his appetite for it, only to completely miss his planned trajectory. Instead half a Bourbon Cream lands right in the middle of Rolando's forehead. Rolando looks most indignant. Ali quickly averts his gaze and places his now free hand gently on Alicia's arm.

'You look awful', he says.

'Th-thanks', says Alicia. 'Why a-are you h-here?'

Ali instructs her to take off her coat, and wraps a picnic blanket around her.

'We saw you disappear, and so set-up camp here yesterday until it got too dark. We only popped down this morning to check if there was any sign of you. To be honest we were about to call it quits and go back home.'

Ali gestures towards two camping chairs and a fold-up table. Alicia wraps the blanket tightly round her; some warmth slowly begins to creep back into her body. Rolando remains at the water's edge looking towards the bridge.

'Where is Patrick?', he calls. 'We assumed he was with you.'

Alicia begins looking around her. She throws off the blanket and runs over to join him upon realising Patrick is not stood with them on the grass.

'He was r-right next to me, I was h-holding on to him!'

'Um… you were holding this', Rolando says, lifting up the heavy damp coat to show her.

He winces, sensing her impending reaction. The familiar pound of panic pulsates through Alicia's chest.

'Oh no no!', she cries.

Alicia leaps back into the stream looking for any sign of him under the bridge. Splashing wildly with all regard for her discomfort gone. She heads back to the spot where he dropped the stick. She looks down at the flowing water. Her insides feel as if they are turning in on themself. A ball of pain grows bigger in the pit of her stomach, making her feel nauseas. In front of her, floating slowly downstream, was one half of the stick closely followed by the other half. Rationally she knew that there was no logical way of knowing if this stick had any connection to anything but she felt its fractured state was a bad omen. She quickly grabs the two pieces, and proceeds to jump in and out of the water, moving from one side of the bridge to the other. She tries dropping the fragmented stick in and out of the stream. But nothing happens. Rolando and Ali watch, their faces pained with concern for their friend.

Alicia's feet are now red raw from her never-ending attempts to jump in and out of the stream, trying desperately to recreate the event that led them to the past. Her body is becoming weary, not even adrenaline can keep her upright much longer. Finally Rolando and Ali manage to persuade her to leave the water and return to dry land; although reluctant to do so, she knew there was no energy left in her body. No other avenue left to try and get back to Patrick. She collapses into the arms of Rolando.

Patrick screams out for Alicia, whilst he frantically scours the water for signs of the stick or anything unusual that hints of a passageway through. It has only been minutes since she vanished but to Patrick it feels like an eternity. He calls out again with tears streaming down his face. His body is so bitterly cold now, he begins to lose feeling in his feet and legs. Using the final strength he has left, he throws himself up onto the bank and collapses in a heap of snow. His eyes slowly begin to close as sobs flow through his body. His usual fighting spirit is frozen, the biting cold numbs his hope and freezes his tears.

His eyes flicker open and shut as he tries to fight succumbing to cold. He notices a shadow slowly spread across his face; forcing his eyes to fully open, he discovers the silhouette of a man standing over him.

'D-dad?', he whispers to the figure.

Patrick feels a large pair of hands grab him under his arms, and pull him from the ground. The man heaves his body up, half over his shoulder. Patrick can feel the man's heart pound and muscles tighten as he tries to manoeuvre through the snow carrying the extra weight of his body.

'It'll be okay lad', the man says softly.

Patrick recognises the voice but he is too exhausted to place it. His eyelids feel heavy. He finally gives up the fight and allows his eyes to close.

CHAPTER 7
FRACTURED

"The only reason for time is so that everything doesn't happen at once." — Albert Einstein

Rolando and Ali are sat in the kitchen with a freshly prepared plate of sandwiches and pot of tea, anxiously awaiting Alicia to emerge with, they hoped, a dry set of clothes on.

'We're definitely all not going mad are we?', Ali whispers to Rolando. 'Alicia wasn't hiding anywhere - she did vanish right?'

Rolando is sympathetic to his husband's doubts; he too experienced some over the course of the last few weeks. The whole situation seems increasingly less comprehensible the more they try to analyse it.

'I never took my eyes off that bridge. And I went under there straight after I saw her vanish in front of my eyes', Rolando replies animatedly.

Ali stuffs part of a sandwich into his mouth, eager to have something to distract him from his thoughts. Rolando continues.

'If we are crazy at least we are all crazy together.'

Ali half smiles as he finishes his sandwich. He looks up at the photos on the wall.

'Wonder what Rhys would make of all this?', he muses.

'Oh he would be loving all this!', Rolando says with a smile. 'Well, except for the fact Patrick is stuck in 1919.'

Rolando's face drops. Both he and Ali look downcast, feeling as if they were somehow letting Rhys down. All three of them had debated what they should do about Patrick. Ali had rung the police but soon put the phone down, once he realised that there was no way of explaining this situation without being dismissed as a crazy nuisance.

'Rhys did love that old bridge though', Rolando says. 'Funny, maybe he knew something about it we didn't.'

Ali silently laughs until he notices Rolando's serious face looking back at him.

'Well', Rolando shrugs.

'What?' Ali responds. 'You don't think he did, do you?'

They both look at one of the pictures of him on the wall, and then turn to face each other again. They both shrug and shake their heads. As Rolando eats a sandwich, Ali looks back at Rhys's picture deep in thought.

'Nah, not possible. Besides Rhys wasn't from these parts he was from London, so I suspect he just fell in love with the quaintness and picturesque scenery - would have been very different to what he'd been used to', Ali concludes.

Rolando does not answer. Alicia finally emerges in dry clothes. Her face is white with worry, and the bags under her eyes are dark and larger than usual. Her hair is uncharacteristically wayward. Rolando gestures for her to have some tea. She slumps down in the chair, feeling both frustrated and exhausted.

'What am I meant to do?', she says feebly.

Rolando and Ali look at each other, hoping one of them has some semblance of an answer. They sit in silence.

'He is in 1919. Freezing. Alone', she says.

Alicia wearily picks up her tea but does not drink it.

'I just pray he has the sense to go back to the farmhouse', she continues.

They sit in silence once again. All three are now staring at their tea but failing to drink it.

'Wait a minute', Rolando says piercing the silence. 'Let's just assume that Patrick is in 1919', he raises his hand up to Ali silently telling him to stay quiet, sensing he was about to interject. 'Well, if he never gets back to the present—'

Alicia gasps. Rolando continues.

'I know if I got stuck in the past I would find a way to leave a message for my family in the future. You know, to let them know what happened to me.'

Ali and Alicia look at one another, and then stare at Rolando. Their eyes widen with hope as the magnitude of what he is saying dawns on them.

'You know what, that is a fair point', Ali says.

Rolando takes a sip of his tea feeling satisfied. Now with increasing confidence he continues.

'And time is in a state of flux right? Time can be re-written, so any changes to the past can have an instant effect on the present'.

Ali looks at him with intrigue.

'In flux? Where are you getting all this from?', he enquires suspiciously.

'That Dr guy', he replies.

Ali rolls his eyes.

'Dr Who?', Ali asks.

Rolando nods his head but is not deterred by Ali's scepticism. He turns towards Alicia. She looks deep in thought, a distinctive crease has appeared in the middle of her forehead as she reflects on Rolando's statements.

'Well', she says. 'Let's start looking.'

She jumps up and grabs her iPad from the side. Rolando and Ali share a surprised glance. Rolando pulls out his phone.

'I'm not really sure where to start looking though', Rolando says.

'What would Dr Who do?', Ali mumbles under his breath as he takes a sip of tea.

Patrick awakes next to a warm fire, covered in multiple blankets. His head throbs from dehydration; he rubs the top of it in a vain attempt to ease the pain as he pulls the blankets off him. His body feels bruised and heavy with exhaustion. As his senses slowly awaken he realises there are hushed voices somewhere nearby.

'And there was no sign of her?', he hears a woman ask someone.

He slowly eases his body out of the chair and turns to see who is behind him. The familiar faces of Gwen, Will and Barnaby all stare back at him. Their faces look sombre and dulled with worry.

'Are you talking about my mum?', he asks.

Gwen nods sympathetically. Will crosses his arms and looks downcast at the floor.

'I looked but I couldn't see her. When did ya last see her?', Will asks, trying to sound as delicate as possible.

'Under the bridge', Patrick says without hesitation.

They all look at him hoping for some further explanation.

'Under the bridge?', Will asks confused. 'Why was she under—'

'Oh I mean.... on top of the bridge', Patrick says, not wishing to elaborate further on any of the events that have unfolded.

'She was er.... I don't know what happened really. Just woke up in the snow', Patrick adds, feeling the skin on his neck prickle. 'The snow was hard to walk in and er.... I think we got tired and lost each other somehow.'

Patrick senses his story was less than convincing. He watches his audience shift uneasily; their silence speaks volumes. Finally someone talks.

'Well', Will says hesitantly. 'I'll obviously go out again and look. Um—'

Whatever Will was about to say he thought better of it and promptly stops speaking. He pulls on his coat; his forehead is wrinkled by troubling thoughts. Patrick wants to tell Will not to bother; that he can look as much as he wants but he will not find her. *Not here anyway,* he thinks. Realising that this may seem an odd thing for a son to say about his mother, he feels little choice but to let Will continue with his search. He watches helplessly as Will heads out of the front door.

'Here, drink this water', Gwen says, appearing next to Patrick and placing a cup of water in his hand.

Patrick begins to sip the lukewarm water; the little sips soon turn into gigantic gulps, and before long the cup runs dry. He underestimated how thirsty he is. His stomach aches dully from the sudden influx of water. Gwen hurries back over to him and replenishes his cup.

'Now don't you worry', she says, 'you can stay here. We'll keep you safe until your mum returns.'

'What if she can't return?', Patrick says without thinking. Gwen meets his gaze, her cheeks look flushed.

'Can't?', she says. 'I'm sure Will will find her.'

Gwen shoots a look towards Barnaby. They share the same thought. *What if she doesn't return.*

Patrick takes his cup to one of the windows, and sips the water more gently. He leans against the windowsill and looks out at the winter wonderland. The white of the snow is dazzling. He shuts his eyes for a moment and imagines what it looks like where Alicia is; green grass, bright yellow flowers, blossoming trees. He opens his eyes again and is blinded momentarily from the brightness of the landscape. *Wait. Is that snow moving?,* he thinks to himself. He watches as a clump of white mass seemingly moves closer. Suddenly a little orange beak appears.

'The duck!', Patrick exclaims.

He runs to the front door and swings it open. There in front of him stands the same duck from before. It lets out a quack and waddles cautiously closer to him. Gwen comes to join him, curious about what Patrick is looking at.

'Huh! Unusual to see a duck round here this time of year. Especially a Call Duck', she says. 'Hang on.'

Gwen disappears back into the house and returns moments later with a slice of bread.

'Here you go', she says handing the bread to Patrick.

Patrick smiles and squats down, he breaks off small chunks of bread and throws it to the grateful duck who enthusiastically scoops up the food.

'Well that's it, I expect that duck will be back everyday now it knows where the food is', Gwen chuckles, feeling endeared by his sudden enthusiasm for the little creature.

'So I wonder if you're stuck here to?', Patrick mutters under his breath to the duck.

Never in his life has he ever felt an affinity towards a duck until now. As strange as it sounds, he feels grateful - almost relieved - to see the duck. Each of them are out of their time; trapped in both a new and old world. Patrick studies its smooth white feathers that are perfectly camouflaged against the snow. He vows to take care of the duck, and dubs it Snowy. Gwen and Barnaby watch Patrick with his new-found friend from the kitchen; they exchange a knowing smile with one another.

'Well', says Barnaby. 'I best get building a duck house.'

Gwen stares into the distance over the top of Patrick's head as he stays crouched on the floor watching Snowy. She looks out across the meadows and wonders where Alicia could possibly be. *What could have happened.* She knows, instinctively, that Alicia would never willingly leave Patrick. Familiar feelings begin to bubble to the surface; the day Eric vanished she felt helpless too. Clueless and lost. Suddenly her small world had opened up; it had felt empty, uncertain and vulnerable. *How can people just vanish?,* she thinks.

Gwen looks back towards Patrick, who is now sat cross-legged in the doorway watching the duck prune itself. Gwen would never want to rob a mother of her child, and she hopes above all else that Alicia will return. But she already knows, without a doubt, that should it not happen then she will protect and care for Patrick as if he were her own. She grips her stomach remembering the child she had lost; the child who never was.

Guilt begins to niggle at Gwen, as she knows a tiny part of her would be grateful to not be alone once Barnaby and Will leave. Grateful that she would have someone who depends on her and needs her. She clears her throat and shakes her head to try and rid herself of this thought. *No,* she thinks to herself. *Let's hope Alicia returns safely.*

The sound of the duck quacking and Patrick's mumbled replies grow distant, as Gwen's mind pulls her back to the time when Eric disappeared. For several minutes she is immersed in her own world, looking back at a time in her life she would rather not remember. She thinks of the last time she saw Eric.

- - - -

Eric drinks the final drops of his tea before setting the cup down on the table. He leans back with his arms outstretched in front of him and lets out a big, loud yawn. The sun has not long risen and, much like any other morning, Eric has been awake to watch it rise. It is his favourite time of day as the world slowly starts to come to life, buzzing with anticipation as a new day of unknown possibilities begins. Today, however, Eric has only one thing on his mind: the peculiar event that took place a few days ago. He has struggled to think of little else since.

He gets up from the chair and heads towards a cabinet on the other side of the room. Pulling open one of the drawers he carefully takes out an object wrapped in a piece of cloth. Glancing around to check that his father has not yet stirred, he proceeds to carefully unwrap the object from its cloth cocoon, revealing a simple stick. He stares at it for a little while, occasionally stroking its surface as if gently petting a newborn kitten. Eric perches on the nearby wooden chair. His thoughts are consumed with questions about the object in front of him and whether it has anything to do with what happened three days ago. He checks the clock on the wall, and realises he must depart to meet Gwen before he heads to work. Reluctant to leave the object unattended, he wraps it back in the cloth and places it in a small sack that contains some of his wood carving tools. Collecting his coat, along with the sack, he makes his way out of his father's house and begins the thirty minute walk to Gwen's cottage.

As he approaches the cottage he spots the familiar figure of Gwen in the distance; the front door is open and she is busying herself in the kitchen. A smile creeps across his face; no matter what life throws his way, he always finds Gwen a stabilising presence. She has no idea what happened a few days ago, and at this point in time Eric did not wish to burden her with it. He is still trying to establish whether he is going mad, and did not want Gwen to come to this conclusion before he had been able to conclude this for himself.

Gwen spots Eric approaching the house and rushes out to greet him. Her arms are open wide ready to embrace him. Eric feels a rush of warmth flood his body. They wrap their arms around each other before Gwen ushers him inside where a hot bowl of porridge awaits. After a few scoops of porridge, Eric notices Gwen staring at him with a look of concern.

'You seem quieter than usual', she remarks.

He swallows another spoon of porridge and shrugs his shoulders in response.

'Do I?', he says. 'Must be tired.'

Gwen nods but is not convinced this is the sole reason for his subdued mood. Eric senses this and tries to to reassure her.

'It's just been a peculiar few days. I'm a little upset Mr Jeffries is cutting down that Rowan Tree - you know the one where the stream meets his farm', he says.

Gwen ponders this for a moment, looking quizzically at Eric.

'Why is that Rowan Tree so important?', she asks.

Eric pushes his empty bowl away from him, and glances down at his bag which contains his carefully wrapped object.

'Oh, no reason. I was just using one of the fallen branches to carve a few things and...', he hesitates for a second. 'And it's just a very beautiful, unusual tree that's all.'

Eric smiles at Gwen and gets up from his seat; he makes his way to the window and stares out across fields.

'It's a damn shame to cut something down in its prime. Especially when it's for his own satisfaction', he continues.

Gwen sees a flash of anger appear across his face as he speaks; she chooses not to press him on the subject any further. Realising his frustrations are getting the better of him, he distracts himself from his thoughts.

'Anyway, I've finished sketching out the design for the house. I think you'll like it', he says in a more cheery tone.

Gwen smiles excitedly.

'I'm sure I will', she says.

'I ought to be going but why don't I take us on a nice picnic down by the stream tomorrow', he says.

'Sounds wonderful', she replies.

He leans over towards Gwen and kisses her gently on the forehead.

'I'll be back soon', he says.

Little does he know, he will never return.

Now that he is out of view from the cottage he pauses for a moment. For the first time in his adult life he chooses to forgo work and instead changes course, heading towards the bridge. As he walks he casts his mind back to the events of three days ago:

- - - -

Eric is sat near the stream, not far from the stone bridge. His father has told him many stories about how his grandfather and great-uncles built this bridge. Perhaps this is why Eric finds himself down here so often; it has become a place of solace. The bridge has also become somewhat of an iconic landmark to the area. He concedes that there is something unusually enticing about the it, but he cannot quite put his finger on why that is.

Eric is perched on a raised piece of earth, carefully whittling a fallen piece of wood from a Rowan Tree. As he peels away the top layer of the stick with his knife, it reveals a smooth velvety-grey surface; it shimmers slightly in the sunlight. He has never seen anything quite like it before. He continues to peel back the top surface, creating a sleek looking stick that more closely resembles a wand with each swipe of his knife. He makes the top a little narrower than the bottom, with a slightly pointed peak. He has no idea *what it is he is making. He decides to allow his hands to work separately from his mind. By the time he is finished he stares at the newly carved object, feeling surprisingly mesmerised by it.*

Noticing one of his feet has fallen asleep, he gets himself up and staggers, as if worse for drink, towards the bridge trying to bring life back to his foot. He leans over the side and looks down at the stream, with the stick still tightly clutched in his hand. He watches the clear water flow beneath where he is stood, and begins to think about his future with Gwen. He wonders whether a few years from now he will be standing here with his own child. He thinks about whether, if given the chance, he would like to know his future or to be left in ignorance. Lost in this deep thought he momentarily loses his grip on the stick and it drops into the stream below. With a gasp he watches it get pulled by the water underneath the bridge. Eric heads down to the edge of the stream waiting for it to reappear with the current. It does not.

'It's just a stick', he says to himself quietly.

Eric picks up his sack and coat, and begins to head back to Gwen's cottage, but a niggling thought won't leave him be; something keeps telling him to go back and get the stick.

'Such nonsense, I will not!', he says to himself as he turns and heads back to the bridge.

If there is one thing to know about Eric it is that he can never ignore a gut feeling. He throws off his shoes and socks, and rolls up his trousers, all the while grateful that it is an unusually warm day for this time of year. He gingerly walks through the cold, clear water and heads under the bridge looking for his prized object.

He wades through the stream trying not to slip on the smooth pebbles beneath his bare feet. He notices a strange looking patch of water but as he steps towards it he becomes aware of the sound of a dog barking. With no sign of the stick, and distracted by the sound of an unknown dog, he heads out from the bridge and steps up onto the grass verge. Shaking his feet dry he looks around and spots a golden Labrador excitedly running about. He does not recognise the dog. It seems to be barking at something on the floor. Eric makes his way towards the dog who becomes more excited as he grows near.

'Ah you want me throw your ball—', Eric stops mid-sentence.

He bends down and picks up the object, which most certainly is not a ball. A bright orange rubber octopus with googly eyes stares back at him.

'Sorry about that', comes the voice of a stranger from behind him. 'I'm walking him for a friend and have been advised that's his favourite toy. He's obsessed with getting people to play fetch with it.'

Eric turns around slowly, still half-looking at the weirdly comical octopus and half-looking at the dog walker. Eric nods and throws the octopus for the dog, who chases after it enthusiastically.

'I've never seen anything quite like that', Eric laughs.

The dog walker goes to speak but is interrupted by a high-pitched squealing sound that grows louder as the dog returns chewing vigorously on the toy's squeaker.

'Good heavens that is..... most peculiar', Eric says completely amused by the fact the strange rubber creature also emits such a loud annoying sound.

'I'm assuming you are not a dog owner', the stranger deduces.

It is only at this point that Eric begins to observe the stranger's attire. A pair of loose fitting blue trousers made of some sort of material he was not familiar with. An oversized striped vest top is tucked into his trousers. Most peculiar of all, a hat that is rounded to his head with a long, stiff flap pointing out on one side. His shoes are like nothing Eric has seen before either; large with white, yellow and blues in. Eric finds the whole ensemble very unusual.

'I've not seen you round these parts before, and I've met most people. I'm Eric.'

He extends his hand out to the stranger who seems a little taken aback.

'Oh yes, hello. I'm Joey. You wouldn't have seen me around, I'm just visiting these parts.'

'Where are you from?', Eric asks.

'Portugal. I know I don't sound Portuguese, mainly because I'm not', Joey replies.

'Gosh you have come a long way then. How long are you here for?'

'Just the weekend, a couple of days.'

'All that way for two days! But the journey alone...'

Joey looks at Eric with some amusement. Suddenly the dog appears with a stick in his mouth, and drops it at Joey's feet. Eric immediately recognises the familiar object.

'Oh I'll take that!', Eric says bending down and beating Joey to it.

Joey looks non-plussed. He considers asking Eric for an explanation but chooses not to. He shakes off his intrigue.

'I'm also going to guess you are not a regular traveller either', Joey says, returning to the previous topic. 'The flight is under three hours. Door to door you're looking at five hours tops', he says.

Eric stares back open mouthed.

'You flew?', Eric asks.

'Er... yes. It is 1995', Joey laughs. 'Anyway, I best go. Nice to meet you Eric.'

Joey walks past Eric, whistling for the dog to follow. The sound of paws running through the grass, and a loud squeaking octopus fade into the distance. Eric remains unmoving and open-mouthed.

'He flew?', he says under his breath.

As Eric replays the whole scene in his head it seems like something out of a strange dream.

'Wait a minute, did you say 1995!?', Eric turns around and calls out after the man but he is long gone.

He glances back down at the stick which feels surprisingly dry. He wonders how the dog managed to retrieve it; and what were the chances it would pick that stick of all sticks. He heads back to the place he left his shoes, sack and coat. To his disappointment he finds they are all missing.

'Surely Joey didn't take them?', he says to himself. 'He seemed so nice.'

He looks around some more in the hope they are just misplaced, but there is no sign of the missing items. Shaking his head in defeat and sadness, he slowly begins to stroll back across the meadows. He starts to ponder his unusual meeting with Joey but is soon distracted by something else unusual; the trees look bigger and bushier, and the woodland seems much more dense too. The whole area feels *slightly different to him. He suddenly comes to an abrupt stop.*

'Gwen?', he shouts.

He stares out towards her cottage, and sees nothing but broken walls and rubble. His world suddenly feels as if it too is in ruin. He breaks into a run and arrives at what would have been Gwen's kitchen. He glides his hands over the cracked stonework noting it looks old and weathered, and that there is no sign of any of the contents of the cottage. A funny feeling fills the pit of his stomach. He breaks into a run once again, this time back towards the bridge. His floppy hair flaps wildly. In his hand, he still clutches the stick tightly.

CHAPTER 8
PAST LIFE

"Lost time is never found again." — *Benjamin Franklin*

Some days have passed since Patrick had been lost. Alicia is once again checking the bridge for any signs that a reunion with her son was possible. She had spent most of her days by this bridge. In her hand she clutches the grey stick, sellotaped back together in a vain attempt this would somehow fix things. Gone were her immaculately manicured nails, perfectly pressed clothes and sleek-backed hair. As long as she had clothes on she cared for little else. She sits down on the grass staring towards the woodland, wishing that a deer had been the only distraction on that fateful day. Alicia spots movement in the corner of her eye; she jerks her head around so quickly a pain surges through her neck. Clutching her neck with one hand, she watches the figure of Rolando run down the hill towards her. She spots some paper in his hand; he is clutching it so tightly his knuckles are as white as the paper.

'Alicia', he calls.

He lands next to her with a bump, and tries to catch his breath.

'What is it?', she asks.

He waves and points at the pieces of paper as he tries to get his breath back.

'I think I've found him - in the past', he says.

Alicia feels a surge of hope rise up in her. Rolando and Ali had spent a great deal of time and money paying subscriptions for access to ancestry archives. She felt a huge sense of appreciation for them. Without her friends she would have truly felt lost. She leans closer to try and see some of the text on the paper.

'Now there is no Patrick Doyle, but there is a Patrick Hunt'. Alicia shakes her head confused.

'But—', Rolando interrupts, 'it is a Patrick Hunt adopted by a Gwen Hunt.'

He holds up one of the pieces of paper to show her.

'And look at the original address', he adds.

Alicia stares in astonishment. It's the farmhouse. She looks up into the distance at the ruined building. Her hand squeezes Rolando's arm, her body overcome with conflicting emotions.

'He made it back. To Gwen. To Will. Oh thank goodness', she says holding her chest with her other hand. 'What else did you find?'

'Crafty little devil he was 'coz he worked in all the rising industries; automobile and telephony. He knows what gets invented and makes money by being where all the action is I guess. I bet they all thought he was some great genius! He made a good living though. Well, here take a look.'

Rolando passes the bits of paper to Alicia, and he watches her study them intently.

'Oh my word', she cries. 'He has kids! And his kids have kids! That means right now...'

She pauses and shuts her eyes, allowing time for her brain to process everything.

'That means as we sit here, I have great grandchildren alive somewhere.'

She pauses to study the pieces of paper further.

'He had his first child in 1929', she says.

After a spell of silence she continues.

'But that means, Patrick is technically de...'

She scans the documents to find what she feared to; his registered death date. Alicia promptly faints. It happens so quickly Rolando does not immediately twig what is transpiring in front of him. He calls out to her and gently taps her face to try and rouse her. Alicia emerges from her unconscious state moments later only to discover Rolando holding her legs up like a giant pair of scissors.

'It helps', he says. 'Gets the blood flow back to your head.'

'Did you learn that on Dr Who too?', she says. Rolando gently returns her legs back to ground.

'Are you okay?', he asks.

'It's just all too much. Such a bittersweet feeling. You find him, which of course is great. But that means right now he is technically', she takes a deep breath in, 'deceased.'

Alicia chokes on her words; both sobbing from joy that he lived a long life, and grief that it has ended.

'It's okay', she says turning to Rolando. 'You go on up to the house. I'm just going to stay here for a little longer. Read a bit more, and just have a moment to think.'

'Okay', Rolando says reluctantly. 'Take some time to read through those', he says gesturing towards the papers in her hand. 'There are some gaps in the story but it does give you an idea of the kind of life he had.'

Rolando pats her on the shoulder as he gets up and makes his way back to the house. He glances back at Alicia a few times, hoping that he has done the right thing. Once Rolando is out of sight, Alicia cautiously gets to her feet, still feeling a little lightheaded. She heads over to the farmhouse, taking the journey slowly; stopping every now and then to re-read the bits of paper. When she eventually reaches the old house she perches on the edge of one of the broken walls. She looks around and tries to imagine which part of the house she is in. She mindlessly caresses part of a brick wall; somehow being here makes her feel closer to Patrick. Alicia tries to imagine what is happening right now in the farmhouse in 1919; a self-contradictory thought if ever she heard of one.

'Excuse me?', says a voice behind her.

Alicia whips her head around startled by the unfamiliar voice, she grimaces and holds her neck again as the pain surges down her shoulder once more. A woman is stood behind her, dressed in a dazzling emerald green linen jacket which make her matching green eyes pop. She was quite a striking woman; similar thick wavy hair to Alicia's, except hers was jet black. Alicia deduced she must be in her 30s.

'Oh I'm sorry', the woman says. 'I didn't mean to startle you. I just wanted to ask if you lived around here?'

'Um sorry, who are you?', Alicia says feeling a little suspicious.

'Oh yes. I'm Rosheen. Rosheen Langley. Strange story - my family, I just discovered, owns these ruins if you can believe it', she says gesturing towards the bits of rubble.

Alicia jumps off the wall.

'When you say your family, who is your family?', Alicia asks eagerly.

'Oh not a family of particular consequence', she replies. 'Well I didn't mean to disturb you. It's just been a bit of a funny day today.'

Rosheen turns to walk away.

'No wait! Please don't go', Alicia says slightly over enthusiastically.

Rosheen turns back towards her, this time it was her turn to look startled.

'Sorry', says Alicia. 'I just mean, can I help you with anything?'

Rosheen studies her for a moment, trying to assess if Alicia can be trusted. She reaches into her pocket and pulls out an envelope.

'This'll probably sound weird but we have had this, not really an heirloom, but an item that has been passed down by my grandfather from his father.' She holds up an envelope. 'We had strict instructions by him not to open it until a specific date.'

Alicia swallows heavily.

'Well technically the date it should have been delivered was several days ago, but my family and I have been at the London Olympics. We decided to call in on our way back. I mean, what harm could a few extra days do?', Rosheen concludes.

Maybe a little bit of harm, Alicia thinks fleetingly.

'Have you seen any of it?', Rosheen asks

Alicia looks confused.

'The Olympics. It's been fantastic!', Rosheen says.

'Oh. Um, no. Didn't realise it was happening', Alicia replies, feeling anxious to return to the original topic.

'Really? Have you been living in the past?', Rosheen says, laughing.

Well technically..., Alicia thinks. She laughs feebly.

'Who was your great-grandfather?', Alicia asks, keen to get back on track.

'A man called Patrick.'

Rosheen reaches into the envelope and pulls out a note, along with another unopened envelope.

'Patrick Doyle Hunt to be exact', she says reading the bottom of the note.

Rosheen looks up and spots the shock on Alicia's face.

'Why, have you heard of him?', she says with surprise.

'Well..', Alicia hesitates. 'Yes he is sort of... he is a relative. Distant relative. Very distant.'

They stare at one another for a moment, both taking in the new knowledge they are related somehow. It slowly dawns on Alicia she is face-to-face with her great-great-granddaughter. Alicia contemplates the fact that to her it has been days without him, but Patrick has lived a lifetime without her. She begins to feel faint again.

'Excuse me one moment', Alicia says.

She lies down on the floor and puts her legs up on one of the bits of rubble. Rosheen looks on feeling both bemused and slightly amused by the spectacle.

'Just feeling a little faint', Alicia explains.

'Oh! Well, are you okay?', Rosheen says unsure what to do.

'So tell me more about this heirloom that isn't an heirloom', Alicia asks pointing towards the envelope.

'Oh, um. Odd story really. My great-grandfather was particularly attached to this old house it seems. He was adopted you see, by the woman who originally lived here. Anyway, it seems my great-grandfather bizarrely wanted this to become a ruin.'

She gestures at the crumbled walls surrounding them, and pauses trying to gauge Alicia's reaction.

'This must be boring for you?', Rosheen says.

'No, no please carry on', Alicia replies, still lying on the floor with her legs up.

'Well funny thing is after remaining sealed for 36 years, I finally opened it as instructed and all that was inside was this note, and a sealed letter.'

She leans over to show Alicia who spins round and jumps to her feet, her body suddenly alive with adrenaline once more. On a simple piece of a paper are the words:

Please ensure the attached letter is placed in the hands of the recipient, unopened.

Attached to the corner of the note is an envelope with a name and address written across it:

Ms Alicia Doyle
Willow Tree Cottage
Tumbridge Valley
Wales

Alicia stares aghast

'Annoyingly no one is at home', Rosheen says. 'Unless you're Alicia.'

Rosheen laughs dismissively and folds the note carefully, placing it back in the original envelope. She sighs, feeling slightly deflated that her quest has been unsuccessful so far.

'I..I... well I am', Alicia says.

Rosheen looks at her. She begins to smile assuming Alicia is joking, but her face soon turns serious when she realises that she is not.

'Seriously? You are Alicia Doyle?'

Alicia nods, her eyes are fixed on the envelope. She desperately wants to rip open the letter.

'I mean I have proof!', Alicia proclaims, worried that her chance to read Patrick's letter may be taken away from her.

'Oh', Rosheen shakes her head. 'Strangely I believe you. Although—'

'What?', Alicia asks trying her best not to sound desperate.

'I was just expecting it to be an old woman for some reason', Rosheen replies.

Rosheen looks at her watch.

'Look I have to go and collect my daughter - I've left her with a friend of mine but we are due to leave again soon.'

'Leave?'

'Yes we live up North.'

Alicia feels a sinking feeling.

'Listen, please come and visit with your daughter. Just call in for a coffee before you leave.'

Alicia glances at the letter sticking out of her pocket. Rosheen hovers between passing it to Alicia or keeping it within the safety of her jacket.

'It's just a little surprising', Rosheen says. 'I was expecting some 90-year old woman. When my great-grandfather wrote this, well, you weren't alive. Or maybe just born?'

Rosheen studies the address on the envelope deep in thought. Alicia shuffles awkwardly unsure what to say.

'Unless your mum or your grandmother were called Alicia Doyle too?'

Alicia shakes her head, feeling a looming sense of disappointment that the letter may not make it into her hands.

'Or... or maybe,' Rosheen looks flustered. 'Let's stroll back towards the house together. My car is parked up that way.'

After what seems like an age to Alicia, they reach the house. The walk had been filled with small talk but both knew that this small talk took place against a backdrop of a more intriguing topic yet to discuss. Much to Alicia's astonishment, Rosheen slowly passes the envelope to Alicia. She tries not to snatch it from her hand such is her eagerness to read it.

'I guess it's too much of a coincidence; it must be for someone in your family somewhere, if not for you. Okay well I'll pop back in before I leave', Rosheen says.

Alicia nods animatedly. Rosheen reaches into her pocket for her phone, but before she has time to say anything Alicia is already blurting out her number. Rosheen offers up a cautious smile.

'Well, I guess I'll see you soon', she says to Alicia.

As soon as Rosheen is gone Alicia tears open the envelope and begins to read. Her eyes already brimming with tears from seeing her son's words on the page. The words of an old man, yet all she hears is the voice of her 11-year old boy in her head.

CHAPTER 9

FAMILY TIES

"All we have to decide is what to do with the time that is given us". — J.R.R. Tolkien

Alicia leans against the bridge looking out over the stream and distant hills; in her hand she clutches the letter from Patrick having not let it out of her sight since she first received it.

Unsure what her own future holds, she seeks comfort from her past. She recalls the fateful day she met Rhys. It had been a slow Saturday morning helping her aunt do a stock-take in her 'Wool and Wares' shop in the local town. Lost in a daydream she became aware of Rhys and Rolando outside the shop window; they were having an animated discussion which she would later learn was about the intricacies of The Matrix film they had just seen. There was no denying Rhys was a handsome man with his floppy brown hair framing his sharp cheekbones, and a cheeky dimple-producing smile; but there was also a compelling charisma about him that drew Alicia in. She watched as they concluded their discussion; both men waved their hands around as if trying to draw their thoughts in the air. She could tell this was a lively friendship, full of strong opinions, humour, and perhaps most importantly, respect.

As they moved away from the window she spotted Rolando's wallet fall from his coat pocket as he fumbled about looking for his mobile phone. Instinctively Alicia rushed out to collect the wallet and called out after them. This simplest of gestures transformed their entire lives.

When Alicia first locked eyes with Rhys, she knew there was something unusual about him. He was like a child experiencing life for the first time; fascinated by cars and planes, mesmerised by video games, adored seeing movies. In fact he seemed completely in awe of even the simplest of things; from a tower block in London to the Severn Bridge gloriously uniting England and Wales. To many it may have seemed he had led a very sheltered upbringing. Yet he was also incredibly mature, kind and intelligent in countless ways; he had made her an exquisite wooden Welsh Love Spoon for their third date. He was an avid reader too with a lust for new knowledge. He wanted to teach history and seemed perplexed that he needed a degree when he already felt he knew so much about the subject he wanted to teach. In the end, he began working at the local shop on a University campus. He took delight in gaining access to some of the student resources, such as books and impromptu chats with the tutors he served. He began writing his own books after Patrick was born. Novels about the 1800s and early 1900s; he wrote so vividly and with such passion and attention to detail.

Rhys had no living family. In fact he spoke so little about his past it had made Alicia a little suspicious at first. As time went on she began to see the pain he was hiding whenever this aspect of his life was touched upon. Alicia decided that, in his own time, he would open up about his past. Although every so often she would feel a tinge of apprehension about what could be causing such a hardened shell to encase his younger life. In the end, a cruel twist of fate meant that he would never have the chance to share his story.

She stares down at her wedding ring made of unique Welsh gold. A smile stretches across her face as she remembers the day he proposed, and the story Rolando had told her afterwards.

- - - -

'Oh this is disastrous!', Rhys says.

'There is no law to say you can't propose when the weather is a bit gloomy', Rolando replies.

'A bit gloomy!? It's thunderstorms and a monsoon outside', Rhys retorts.

'How does this affect you proposing to Alicia?', Rolando asks.

The whole plan is based outside', Rhys says.

Rolando watches his friend pace the floor. He did feel a little sad for Rhys, as he knew he had been planning this proposal meticulously for months.

'Well we will just have to move it inside', Rolando says.

Rhys continues to pace, shaking his head. Rolando takes a swig of whiskey.

'Let's not lose sight of what is important here. Yes, you had a lovely plan all sketched out. But at the end of the day, if you proposed to Alicia right now as she walked through this door, the end result would still be the same', Rolando said confidently.

'Oh no what do you mean!?', Rhys's face becomes stricken with panic.

'I mean she would say yes either way, you wally', Rolando says through laughter.

Rhys manages a feeble smile; he was a nervous wreck already.

'You don't understand. A proposal needs to be done with much ceremony and fanfare. It takes months of planning', Rhys says firmly.

Suddenly Alicia bursts through the door holding a box of cup cakes; she has a huge grin on her face. Rhys is struck by how beautiful she looks as the sunlight streams in and shines on her like a spot light.

'Guess what?', she says excitedly.

'Will you marry me?', Rhys blurts out before he realises what he is doing.

Rolando almost drops his glass of whiskey in amazement. He laughs and rolls his eyes as he watches the scene unfold in front of him. Rhys and Alicia stare at each other in shock.

'Yes!', she cries.

Rhys regains his composure having shocked himself with his spontaneous proposal. He rushes over and gives Alicia a hug.

'Well that took a surprising turn', Rolando says to Rhys.

'Life is short, you have to seize the day', Rhys says with a cheeky smile and a wink.

Rolando lets out a snort of laughter at his friend's sudden change in attitude.

'You ought to have seen what he's been like the last few weeks. A total bag of nerves!', Rolando says to Alicia.

'Who me? Nervous? No. I was completely calm', Rhys says.

'Oh and guess what?', Alicia says. 'I'm pregnant'.

Rhys faints.

- - - -

Alicia moves her arm across the wall of the bridge and seeks out the carving of his initials *R.S.* an all too familiar sensation beneath her fingertips. One day he had candidly said to her that he had etched his initials here to 'leave evidence of his presence'. Alicia never thought about this story much until now; as she replays the memory in her mind she can see the emotion in his eyes. Sometimes he acted as if he was only passing through, or was somehow out of place here. *Why was he so emotional?*, Alicia asks herself. A niggling feeling begins to tingle in her gut. *Did he know something about the bridge she didn't?* She closes her eyes and rewinds her mind, pressing play at every memory of Rhys talking to her about where he was from, how he came to be in this area, and his passion for buying Willow Tree House when it was built. She was surprised at what limited information she knew about Rhys; so consumed was she by living with him in the present she had acquired few puzzle pieces about his past to be able to form a clear picture.

It was Rhys who had picked out Willow Tree House as their future home. It was Rhys who had only wanted to live within this specific area. It was Rhys who had organised many weekends, prior to buying the house, taking picnics on the meadow by the stream. It was on this bridge where Rhys would spend many an hour whenever life got too much and he needed to think. In fact, now Alicia begins to pull out all of these memories and piece them together, it begins to build an image of a man who was almost obsessed with this place. *Why?,* she thinks. *Could it be for the same reason I am now obsessed with this place?* She shakes her head dismissively. Lack of sleep and stress was pulling her brain in all directions.

'Alicia?'

The sound of Rolando's soft voice calling out to her raises her spirits momentarily.

'How long have you been out here?', he asks.

Alicia shrugs her shoulders and looks towards her watchless wrist.

'I was lost thinking about Rhys actually', she replies.

Rolando leans on the bridge next to her and smiles. 'Impossible not to miss him', he says.

Alicia nods thoughtfully. Her eyes glaze with grief.

'Did you ever notice how attached he was to this place?', Alicia asks.

Rolando takes a minute to digest this question. Alicia can tell he is flicking through his memories like a picture book.

'Well', he says finally, 'I guess he was very taken with this place. Seemed to feel at home here I suppose.'

Alicia grunts in agreement but with an undertone of scepticism. Rolando picks up on this and turns to face her.

'Why, what are you thinking?', he asks.

Alicia shrugs her shoulders again, unsure how to put her scattered thoughts into fully-formed sentences.

'It's just he never spoke about his life before he met either of us—'

She cuts herself off abruptly and dithers, whilst trying to read whether Rolando was already guessing her next words.

'It makes me wonder that's all. Was there something about this place?', she says tapping the edge of the bridge with her fingers. 'Something that he wasn't telling us.'

Rolando nods and raises an eye brow realising what Alicia is insinuating.

'And I guess the main reason you would hide something is either because it is so horrible or shameful, or maybe in this case because you think no one would believe you', Alicia says looking at Rolando expectantly.

Rolando plans his next words carefully in silence. He looks down at the carved initials which Alicia gently strokes once more with her fingers.

'There is something I never told you', he says. 'I was younger at the time, and it felt like the right thing to do. I wanted to give Rhys a chance, he seemed so broken when I met him.'

Alicia straightens up and turns to face Rolando. Her cheeks flush red in anticipation of the impending revelation. Rolando breathes heavily.

'When I met Rhys he said he had run away from home, and that he was unable to go back. He wouldn't tell me anymore details, other than the fact that he hadn't done anything wrong and just needed help to make a new life for himself. Well, I put him up on my couch for the first few months and he always seemed like such a good, caring guy. But he had no papers; no ID; nothing.'

Rolando pauses and shuffles awkwardly on his feet, failing to meet Alicia's gaze.

'So I helped him. A friend of a friend of a friend....you know, got him some papers.'

Rolando feels his face getting hotter. He raises his head and looks at Alicia, who is staring back at him. Her face unmoving.

'So was his real name Rhys Smith?', Alicia asks finally, her voice cracking slightly. 'Was he even from London?'

'I never knew what is actual surname was. But his first name was Eric. I don't know where he was from.'

Alicia slumps back into the wall of the bridge, allowing it to take her weight as her mind weighed heavy with an influx of thoughts. Rolando stands frozen to the spot, unsure what he should do next.

'I'm not cross with you Rolando', she says. 'You helped your friend build a life for himself.' She lets out a big sigh. 'It's just I feel like I never knew who he was.'

'Listen, you know he was a great father and husband.'

Rolando places a comforting hand on her shoulder.

'Eric?', Alicia mutters. 'I can't imagine him being an Eric.'

Alicia feels as if a memory is trying to claw it's way to the surface. She thinks of Gwen for a moment but is unsure why. Rolando interrupts her thinking.

'Well to us he was and always will be Rhys. That's who he wanted to be', Rolando says delicately.

After a brief pause Alicia decides to just say what is on her mind.

'Everyone has a past. What if his was just, you know, quite bit further in the past', she says.

Rolando nods absentmindedly, whilst surmising if he agrees with this statement.

'Well', Rolando says, 'let's say Rhys did come from the past. If he was stuck here, then he managed to create a pretty good life for himself. So does it matter?'

Rolando holds his breath slightly, unsure how these words will hit Alicia's ears. Rolando leans over the edge of the bridge and thinks of his friend, recounting the words Alicia just told him.

'It did always feel like he was looking for something', Rolando says.

Alicia turns towards him.

'Do you know what, that's true. It was as if he was trying to find something whenever we were here. Just something in his manner, the way he was always slightly on edge as if on the lookout for something', she says.

Rolando bows his head and shuts his eyes for a second, his mind overloaded with thoughts.

'I best go', she says forcing a smile. 'I am expecting visitors.'

<hr />

Two rapid knocks on the front door reverberate through the house. Alicia gets up from her chair, and quickly wipes away her tears before pushing Patrick's letter back into her pocket. She opens the door to find Rosheen staring back at her with a warm smile, although her eyes flicker with nerves. She has her arm around a young girl, perhaps 7 years old Alicia guesses, with ringlets of beautiful auburn hair and a face adorned with freckles The girl smiles shyly at Alicia, clutching a book like a shield.

'Hi again', says Rosheen. 'Oh this is my daughter, Alicia'. Alicia is slightly taken aback. Rosheen turns to her daughter.

'This is also Alicia', she says. 'I told you it was cool name!'

Rosheen turns back to Alicia.

'We actually call her Lishy. No idea why. It just seems to have stuck', Rosheen tells her.

'Well please do come on in. I have cookies', Alicia says, looking at Lishy.

A smile creeps across the girl's face. Alicia feels a little overcome with coming face-to-face with yet another generation of her family; this time her great-great granddaughter.

'What's that?', Alicia asks Lishy pointing towards the book she is carrying.

Lishy holds the book up, coyly hiding her face behind it.

The Art of Magic.

'Oh magic!' Alicia says reading the cover. 'I may have to read that later', she whispers to Lishy.

Lishy lowers the book and smiles at her; she begins eating a cookie. Rosheen turns to Alicia.

'So I am dying to know - what was in the letter?', Rosheen asks.

In that moment Alicia realises she has not come up with any sort of cover story. Her mind whirls a millions miles an hour. *Should I be honest? Will she think I'm crazy?,'* she thinks to herself. Finally she decides to err on the side of caution.

'Oh your father knew me, I mean my mother - grandmother', she says slightly unconvincingly. 'Long ago. They got separated from each other and were never able to reconnect.'

Alicia quickly changes the subject, pushing a cup of tea towards Rosheen.

'So tell me about yourself - you live up North you say?'

Rosheen parks her curiosity about the letter, although Alicia suspects it will resurface again at some point.

'Yes I live up there with my husband. My parents are also up there too', Rosheen responds.

'So tell me a bit more about your family. Your mum, and grandmother. Just curious, you know, because er.... our families have overlapped', Alicia asks.

Alicia was eager for the names written on the pages of the family-tree that Rolando had found, to be bought to life. She soon learnt that Patrick's daughter, Lillian born 1929, became a nurse and saved the life of her future husband Albert. They then went on to have a child called Catherine in 1941 who became a theatre star, and a part-time fortune-teller; Alicia made a note to learn some more about her. Then Rosheen was born in 1979, and she decided to become a carpenter.

'I just love making things', enthused Rosheen. 'And I thought, why not become a carpenter - make a decent living doing something I enjoy.'

Alicia sat back to collect her thoughts for a moment. *Wow,* she thought. *Three generations of my family.* She looks over at Lishy. *Four generations.* It is astonishing; she had gained an entire tree of grandchildren within weeks.

'Oh one other thing to know about Lillian, she not only saved the life of her future husband, but she saved the life of the would-be Major Linton', Rosheen says rather proudly.

'Who?', Alicia asks.

'Oh I assumed you may have heard of him as he was from this area. Think there is a memorial dedicated to him in town. He famously stopped someone from assassinating the Prime Minister in 1951. If Lilian hadn't saved Major Linton, then he would never have been there to stop that from happening. Fate is funny like that', Rosheen says.

Alicia leans back into her chair, and digests this new nugget of information.

'How extraordinary', she replies.

Soon the minutes turn into hours, and the threesome find themselves huddled around the table learning magic tricks from Lishy's book. Lishy roars with laughter as she watches Alicia attempt to make a coin appear behind Rosheen's ear. Alicia moves her hand away from Rosheen's ear loudly declaring:

'Abracadabra!'.

A coin falls from her sleeve and proceeds to hit Rosheen in the face. Lishy curls up into a ball of laughter. Alicia looks at Rosheen apologetically.

'You can keep the coin', Alicia says. 'Compensation.'

Rosheen smiles, rubbing her nose that stings slightly from the coin impact.

'It's weird', Rosheen says once the laughter has died down. 'Feels like I've known you before. Does that sound odd?'

Alicia shakes her head. She glances towards the picture of Rhys and Patrick, her heart cries a little. *It's so bittersweet,* she thinks. Longing for her son to be back, but also marvelling in the afternoon spent getting to know her great-granddaughter.

'Oh gosh, do you have a children?', Rosheen asks, noticing the array of pictures on the wall.

Alicia suddenly feels a heaviness in her chest. Once again, she finds herself unsure what to say.

'Yes. Well. I', she stumbles over her words. 'My husband and son - I lost them.'

Rosheen looks visibly moved. She gets up from her seat and puts her arms around Alicia.

'They're never really lost', Rosheen says. 'Just temporarily parted from us. Well, that's what I believe anyway.'

Rosheen does her best to sound reassuring, but worries she sounds silly. Alicia smiles and nods at her, resisting the urge to crumble into pieces.

'Well if you ever feel the need to talk about it, I'm a much better listen than I am talker', Rosheen says.

'Actually', says Alicia. 'Why don't you both stay for dinner?'

CHAPTER 10

IN WITH THE OLD

"Only in the darkness can you see the stars". - Martin Luther King Jr

Patrick stares at his reflection in the water. Almost two months have dragged by and there has been no sign of Alicia. His hair is now much longer than it was; he looks at the curly mop upon his head that frames the face staring back at him through the water. Gwen has promised to cut his hair later today, having finally agreed to let her do it. With Snowy loyally by his side, he sits down on the crisp morning grass mindlessly throwing stones into the stream.

'Alright?', comes a voice from behind.

Merlin, the strawberry-blonde boy, sits down next to him. He pulls half a jam sandwich from his coat pocket and gives it to the duck.

'Who walks around with a jam sandwich stuffed in their pocket?', Patrick says, both amused and a little disgusted.

Merlin proudly points at his chest in response.

'What pockets are for ain't it', he refutes.

Patrick smirks and looks back towards the water watching it ripple as he launches another stone. Hanging out with Merlin by the stream had become somewhat of a routine. Patrick found him comically straightforward; Merlin wasted no time with things like small talk, or considering the consequences of his actions. He was clumsy and prone to getting himself into avoidable predicaments. He was actually a refreshing distraction to Patrick. He liked that Merlin seemed to show no curiosity about how Patrick suddenly arrived here with no family.

'Oh here she comes!', Merlin says, rolling his eyes. 'Miss bossy-boots'.

Patrick turns and sees Catherine, Merlin's older sister, skipping across the grass towards them. Patrick reflects on how much he enjoys spending time with her, so much so he is willing to overlook her incessant need to organise his life. He watches her straight bob of hair flap about as she skips; her smile radiates out towards him and he finds himself grinning cheek-to-cheek as she nears.

'What you smilin' about?', Merlin asks him with a look of confusion.

'Oh, nothing', Patrick says quickly, blushing a little.

Patrick turns away and pretends to be looking at something in the distance. Catherine lands down beside him with an enthusiastic thud.

'Should've known I'd find you two here', she says.

'It's where we come and do our thinking ain't it', Merlin says, nudging Patrick.

Patrick looks towards Merlin in amusement; he had never struck Patrick as being much of a deep-thinker, so this came as news to him.

'Well anyway', Catherine continues. 'Mum and dad say you can come over for dinner later if you want?'

Patrick places his hand on his stomach, unsure why he suddenly feels a strange flutter in his belly. He rubs his stomach in the hope this will make the feeling disappear.

'Er... yeah sure. Okay', Patrick says sheepishly.

'Goodo!', Catherine says, feeling jollied by his reply. '5'o'clock. Don't be late. Both of you.'

She gives Merlin a stern look.

'What?', Merlin says, raising his hands in the air.

Catherine studies the stream, watching the water navigate its way at speed down towards the bridge. She turns her attention back towards Patrick.

'Why do you come here so much?', she asks.

Patrick is caught off guard by this question, despite it being a perfectly reasonable one. He wonders whether one day he will ever be able to tell her the real reason why. For now, he says the only explanation he can think of.

'Water is nice er... to look at', he responds, and immediately regrets his answer.

Catherine looks back at him in silence for a moment, her eyes squinting as if trying to decipher what he said.

'I....see', she says slowly. 'I was just wondering because you always seem to be down here, looking around that bridge.'

'And you always seem to be around here staring at Patrick', Merlin interjects with an air of smugness.

Catherine's face turns a deep shade of red. She turns towards Merlin and shoots him a look of annoyance.

'No.. I... oh shush, Merlin!', she says feeling flustered.

Merlin snorts out a laugh. Patrick is unsure whether to feel amused like Merlin, or flustered like Catherine. He attempts to be a mixture of the two, and the result is an awkward mess of half- smiles and chin rubbing.

'Well what's with all these questions. I already said, we come here to think', Merlin says. He leans back resting on his hands looking proud of himself. 'It's what men do.'

Catherine nearly chokes on her words as they surge out of her mouth.

'Men!? Firstly, you are 11, Merlin. Secondly, what do you think happens to women? They come down here and empty their brains? Thinking isn't exclusive to men but being an idiot is exclusive to you', she says in protest.

Merlin smiles, his mission is accomplished. His sister is successfully annoyed. Snowy gives Merlin a quick peck as if in punishment; Catherine smiles.

'So are you staying in the area permanently?', Catherine asks Patrick.

Never has a single question caused such an extreme reaction to his body; his face drains of colour, he feels sick, and he crosses his arms tight over his chest suddenly feeling the need for a hug.

'Er.... maybe. I don't know', he says quietly.

Catherine stares at him curiously. She can sense this question has made him uneasy.

'Well', she says trying to sound reassuring. 'I for one hope you do stay. It'll be fun.'

Patrick feels a little rallied by this comment. No one wants to be somewhere where they feel unwanted, and between Gwen and Catherine he has begun to feel a small sense of belonging.

'It's just a bit different you know? From where I'm from', Patrick says.

'Where are you from?' Catherine asks.

Patrick rolls his eyes at his own stupidity, realising he has walked himself into this awkward situation.

'Just somewhere a long way from here', he says.

He knew that Catherine would not find this answer satisfactory.

'Well what's different about it?', she persists.

'Oh', says Patrick with a deep intake of breath. 'There were just more things to do. Like games called video games, you could play them without leaving your room. And like those things you call moving pictures, we could sit in our room and watch lots of different ones whenever we wanted'.

Catherine considers this information for a moment.

'So what you're saying is you didn't leave your room?', she muses.

Patrick does not know how to respond to this. Strangely she is partly right. But hearing her say it back to him makes it sound silly. Still trying to decipher what Patrick has just told her, Catherine stretches her arms up in the air and yawns.

'Right well I best go. I promised to help with the dinner', she says.

She skips off once more into the meadow. Patrick watches her bounce out of sight.

'Don't worry - one day she will move out and you won't have to deal with her ever again', Merlin says.

Patrick hopes he is wrong; he begins to wonder what the future has in store for him. Each day he feels the burden of knowing what's coming; a war being the most prominent thing on his mind. He wished he had listened a little more in his history lessons, never once imagining he would become part of it.

Patrick decides to put the new-found knowledge that his friend is a deep-thinker to the test.

'Er, Merlin? Do you think you'd rather live in the past or the future?', Patrick asks.

Merlin launches a stone in the air but somehow it fails to even make it to the water, instead it lands a mere 30cms away from him on the grass. Merlin seems more confused by this than he does about Patrick's question.

'I live in the present', he responds confidently. Patricks smiles feebly.

'Well yeah, I know. But I mean, what if you got stuck in the wrong time. What would you do?'.

Merlin ponders this for a second.

'Simple', he says. 'Just change the clock to the right time'.

Patrick was not expecting this response.

'Hmm. But what I mean is— never mind', Patrick says, deciding not to pursue this subject any further.

Merlin rolls onto his front and pushes himself up off the grass; unbothered by the bits of dirt now attached to his clothing.

'You comin'?', asks Merlin.

Patrick shakes his head. Merlin heads off back towards his home, making a few detours on the way no doubt. Patrick supposes he will likely arrive before Merlin does for dinner.

Patrick tousles his hair with his hand, feeling pleased it will soon be short again. For some reason he did not want to change a single hair on his body, as if in some strange way this would affect him returning to his normal life. It is only now he realises that this *is* his life, and the only way for it to become normal is to live it that way. *I can't wait for video games to be invented,* he thinks to himself.

People are beginning to ask questions about him; he had overheard Gwen tell someone he is an orphan and that she has taken him in. *I suppose I am an orphan,* he thinks. Although he resents being thought of in that way. Yet he cannot help but feel a profound sense of gratitude towards Gwen. After all, without her he would have nowhere warm to sleep at night. No food to eat. No one to care about him. She never admits it but he can tell she enjoys having him around to make a fuss over, having been a childless mother for so long.

He stares at the bridge. *Come on Mum,* he wilfully wishes. Like all of the days that have passed before this one, no sign of his mother comes. No hint. No clue. No inkling of anything more than a normal bridge and stream. He looks downcast as he leaves his place by the water's edge; having been sat there for so long, too long perhaps, his bottom now feels numb. He stretches his arms and legs in a bid to awaken his muscles from their sleepy state. One final look back at the bridge, *still nothing.* With a heavy heart he makes his way back to the farmhouse. *Back home,* he thinks. It sounds weird in his head. *But I better get used to it.*

As he approaches the house he can see Gwen busy in the kitchen. She is a woman who is forever busy; always finding something to do.

'Oh hello dear, did you have a nice time with Merlin?', she asks as Patrick enters the room.

He nods, and glances at the table where a pair of scissors and towel are already laid out in preparation for his hair cut.

'Do you mind if I go over to his house for dinner?', he asks.

'Of course not. Will Catherine be there?', Gwen says with a coy smile.

Patrick rolls his eyes and shakes his head playfully.

'Well best tidy this up then', she says pointing towards his hair.

As Patrick takes a seat at the table, he thinks how incredibly average this scene is. It is as if he has slotted into 1919 with no consequence. Somehow he expected something incredible to happen; a person from the future colliding with the past ought to happen with much more fanfare, he ponders.

'You know I met Eric when I was about your age', Gwen said.

Patrick nods causing Gwen to almost cut half his hair clean off.

'Er... best you keep your head still', she says, relieved to have avoided disaster.

'What was he like?', Patrick asks.

Gwen smiles broadly as she thinks back to some happier times.

'He was very kind and generous. Very creative. He made some of this furniture actually.'

Patrick looks around the room.

'Oh is that why the chairs are all mismatched?', he asks.

Gwen bursts out laughing.

'Oh I meant that in a good way. It's nice that not everything is the same', he says quickly.

Patrick watches his freshly cut hair drop to the floor.

'My dad liked to make things too', he says. 'He made me my first skateboard. Well, once he worked out what one was'.

Gwen pauses from cutting his hair and looks up at the ceiling, mouthing the word *skateboard* to herself.

'What is a skate, board?', she asks curiously.

'Oh', Patrick says as he realises his mistake. 'Um.. it's like a board on some wheels that you can stand on. You kinda push yourself forward with one foot and then stand on it and ride it'.

He could tell Gwen was working hard to imagine what this contraption was.

'Wow', she said finally. 'What a funny and clever idea.'

Patrick takes a big gulp. Had he just inadvertently made his dad the inventor of the skateboard? If he had he would add it to the growing list, having already accidentally made his dad the writer of several songs of The Beatles. He found himself singing them at times without realising it, they were a comforting reminder of his dad and brought him brief moments of joy when he got lost in their melodies. He was pretty sure he heard Merlin humming the tune of All You Need is Love the other day. *Must be more careful,* he thought. Gwen suddenly starts whistling the tune of Love Me Do; Patrick quickly interrupts.

'So, Eric sounds fun', Patrick says, trying to find a safe topic.

'Yes. Sounds like Eric and your dad would have been the best of friends', Gwen says cheerily but with a pinch of sadness.

The room falls silent except for the sound of the scissors snipping away at Patrick's hair. Patrick missed Will and Barnaby, and was still unsure why they were forced to leave this area. It frustrated him. The house seemed bigger without them. If he left too, he wondered how Gwen would cope with the silence.

Suddenly there is a loud flapping sound outside. Snowy flashes past the window en route to land. Patrick hears him scratching and pecking on the other side of the door.

'I wonder what has got that duck so riled up', Gwen says.

Patrick shuts his eyes and thinks back to the moment that his dad had surprised him with a new skateboard. A smile creeps across his face.

- - - -

'Surprise', Rhys cries.

Patrick takes a few steps back in shock, as Rhys springs out from behind his bedroom door. Patrick, having just returned from school, had been lost in thoughts about his boring day confined to the classroom. Rhys proudly holds out a new skateboard.

'Is that for me?', Patrick excitedly asks.

'Sure is', says Rhys. 'I made it myself.'

'No way! You made this?'

Patrick studies the shiny new object in awe.

'Yep, took me a while. I also put your initials on it', Rhys says, gesturing towards the bottom of the board.

'It was meant to be done in time for your 9th Birthday; sorry it's a little late', Rhys says.

Patrick is too busy marvelling at his new gift to notice what Rhys said, or even care that it is a few months after his birthday.

They eagerly make their way outside to test out the new set of wheels. Rhys watches Patrick effortlessly glide up and down the path. He delights in the sight of his son's happiness; his brain boggles at the notion that Patrick was born 112 years after he was. Rhys's mind drifts into thoughts about how unexpectedly his life has turned out. For what feels like the hundredth time, he wonders what he would do if he was ever able to return to his old life; and for the hundredth time he is unable to give a definitive answer. The emotion he feels when he contemplates any scenario that would involve leaving his son behind overwhelms him. Yet even after all this time, he still feels a step out of time; like he is a visitor passing through on a temporary visa.

'And it's red just like the car', Patrick says, pointing at the skateboard.

Rhys re-focuses his mind.

'Oh yes. Got to coordinate', Rhys says.

Rhys looks at the red MG parked on the drive; another impulse buy of his. It would be his summer project. He had visions of taking Alicia down to the coast in it, with the top down and their hair flying all over the place.

'Why don't you have a go?', Patrick asks, as he hands the skateboard over to him.

Rhys is briefly flummoxed by this question. It had not occurred to him to actually try it; his sole focus had been to build it.

'Go on!', Patrick encourages.

Rhys places his feet on the board with much trepidation. Patrick is giving him several instructions, but he only hears half of them. He uses his right foot to push against the ground and propel the board forward.

'Ahhhhh!', Rhys shouts.

His left leg turns to jelly. His right leg is unable to coordinate its movement and hangs in an ungainly manner. His arms fly around wildly. Rhys makes a doomed decision; he concludes it is best to finish the rest of the journey on all fours. Bending over and bringing his hands down to grip the front of the board, he finds himself in an instant roly-poly. He lands on his back hitting the ground with a thud, just in time to see the skateboard fly over him.

Patrick runs over to him in fits of laughter.

'That was brilliant', Patrick says.

'That was wild', Rhys replies breathlessly.

'You only went the length of the car though', Patrick says. 'Right, I'm gonna get mum.'

Patrick runs off, still full of giggles.

Rhys gets up and rubs the base of his back, which feels sore from its abrupt contact with the hard pavement. He heads over to collect the stray skateboard which has landed in the middle of a large patch of forget-me-nots. As he picks up the board a cluster of the flowers gets tangled up in the wheels. Pulling free the final forget-me-not, and tossing it to the floor, a sudden feeling tugs at Rhys's heart. A feeling that often visits him; a sense of guilt for finding joy in a life without the people he loved from his past. Recently discovering that his old fiancé lived and died alone had profoundly impacted him; he almost wished that he had never looked up her details. Ignorance is sometimes a key ingredient of contentment, he had decided.

'What is this I hear about you performing summersaults on a skateboard!?', Alicia calls out, as she marches out of the house.

'Well I think I did rather well', Rhys replies.

Alicia chuckles.

'Well, given the demonstration Patrick just gave me, I would have to disagree', Alicia says.

Rhys's smile turns into a grimace as a jolt of pain surges up his back. He groans and rubs the base of his spine again. Alicia looks at him sympathetically, but a smile still lingers.

'I'll get you some ice', she says.

Rhys watches Alicia disappear back into the house. He wonders how he managed to find two women, from different times, who were both willing to marry him.

'So what did you play with when you were young?', Patrick says, brushing the dirt from his skateboard.

'Oh, well... I had a few favourite things. A set of soldiers - I loved those', Rhys says.

'Oh you mean like those little plastic soldiers in a bucket?'

'No, cardboard ones', Rhys says.

Patrick looks confused.

'Cardboard?' Patrick says. 'Why not plastic?'

'Fancy a stroll to the bridge?', Rhys asks, changing the subject.

Patrick shrugs and nods his head; his dad seemed to find the strolls down by the bridge much more interesting than he did, although Patrick did not mind too much. They would often play football down on the meadow.

'I'll just grab my coat', Rhys says.

As Rhys turns to walk away, Patrick tugs at his arm.

'Thanks', Patrick says, holding up the skateboard.

Rhys smiles.

'We can go the skateboard park on the weekend if you like', he replies.

'Awesome!', Patrick says with excitement.

Rhys walks to the garage to grab his jacket that is hanging next to the workbench. Rhys pulls on his coat and turns to leave, but pauses for a moment to brush away the remnant of one of the forget-me-nots stuck to his trouser leg. He watches the blue petal drift away; a gentle breeze sweeps it underneath a cabinet. Rhys's focus shifts from the floor to one of the cabinet drawers. Glancing behind him to check no one is around, he reaches behind the cabinet and pulls out a key and uses it to unlock the top drawer. He takes out a small black sketchbook, and brushes away some dust from the cover. It has been a while since he had looked at it. The pages of the book contain simple, yet beautiful, pencil drawings he had done several years ago. His eyes twinkle with water at the image of a young woman with a warm smile and gentle eyes; and an older man with similar features to Rhys. This was the closest Rhys had to a modern photo album of his old life. Finally his eyes come to rest on a page that has a sketch of a stick, with a distinctive knot in the middle of it. He studies it.

'What happened to you?', he whispers.

His face creases from concentration as the memory of the last time he saw it begins to fade with time. He gently traces the lines and shapes on the page with his finger, as if trying to commit every detail to memory. After observing the image for a few moments more he closes the book, and locks it away again; making sure to tuck the key back out of sight. Alicia suddenly enters the garage, clutching a shopping list in one hand and a pack of ice in the other.

'Oh, before you go down to the bridge, I don't suppose you would pop to the shop with me?', Alicia asks.

'Sure' Rhys says. 'The bridge can wait.'

Rhys glances at the locked drawer, and places the ice pack on his back.

'It's a bit bruised that's all', he says turning back to Alicia.

'Rolando has just popped round and said he will stop with Patrick for a bit. They're playing on that old Gameboy you bought. It looks so old-fashioned now, not sure what made you buy it', Alicia says, smiling.

Rhys laughs.

'Looks futuristic to me', he says.

He still feels like he is catching up with all of the technological advances. The house brims with old and new gadgets - although they all feel new and cutting-edge to him. He still enjoys the mechanics of a cassette tape in a Walkman much to his son's amusement. Patrick has progressed on to a little handheld device called an iPod, but Rhys cannot get his head around how all of the music is able to fit on such a small object. Besides, Rhys enjoys the thrill of winding the tape of a cassette back in without breaking it and losing his music forever; when he succeeds, he feels like a true mechanical genius.

'Ooh, let's get everyone pizza', he says eagerly.

'You are obsessed with pizza', Alicia says, feeling amused.

'Amazing invention', he replies, with a wide grin on his face.

'I can't believe you never had pizza growing up', Alicia says.

'It was something we never came across.'

'There was so much you never came across', Alicia replies.

Rhys chooses not to respond to this comment, already feeling a little awkward. He often felt awkward when it came to any conversation about his childhood; to everyone here his upbringing always sounded very shielded. He sometimes contemplated telling Alicia his journey from past to present but always managed to talk himself out of it, reasoning that she would never believe such an extraordinary tale.

As Rhys climbs into the car next to Alicia, he resigns himself to the fact that he will probably be the only person in the world who ends up lost in time due to the questionable powers of a Rowan Tree; a tree that is now long gone.

As he drives through the country lanes heading towards the local town, Alicia gently places her hand on Rhys's leg. She looks over at him and cannot help but take a moment to admire his perfectly chiselled face, piercing eyes and his comically floppy hair. Time has been kind to him, she thought. He has hardly aged at all since she first met him.

'We're really lucky you know. I don't think there is anything I would change right now about our life', she says softly.

Rhys thinks about her words for a minute or so; they seem to have a deep, reassuring effect on him. He often found himself doubting his life choices, overthinking all of the different paths he could have taken; but somehow Alicia seemed to say the right thing, in the right moment, and those doubts would get buried away again.

'Yes, I think you're right', he says.

His mind flashes with images of his life; past and present. Two very different chapters, but both full of friendship, love and meaning.

'I am the lucky one', he mouths quietly.

Rhys reflects on how he has been carrying his regrets and guilt around with him like a heavy bag on his shoulders; dragging him down, affecting everything he does, pulling his focus away from just living in the present. He knows that he could never have predicted that his life would toke the turn it did. He knows there are things he has no power to change, even if he wanted to.

I need to put down the bag, he thinks to himself.

He turns up the radio and begins rapping badly to a Jay-Z song. Alicia stares at him with a look of both amusement and annoyance in equal measure.

Rhys turns onto the main road towards the town, for what will be the last time.

And just like that, Rhys's time is up.

CHAPTER 11
THE CHOICE

"Who controls the past, controls the future: who controls the present controls the past." — *George Orwell*

licia unfolds the letter. Her eyes fall upon the date at the bottom again: *1979. The year I was born,* she thinks. A tsunami of emotion consumes her, and she breaks into waves of sobs. She cradles the letter in her hand to shield it, not wishing to let the ink run away with her tears. After several minutes she refocuses her eyes to read the letter once more, despite having already read it 25 times.

Mum, For you it has probably only been days since you returned to the future. For me, it has been 60 years living in the past. I'm sure you have been frantically trying to find a way to get me back. I have returned to the bridge most days, so I think it is safe to assume you were never able to make it back through to the past. I know how much this will be hurting you, and I have always hated the thought of you being alone and worrying about me. This is why I have done everything I could to make sure this letter reaches you.

Please do not worry about me. I have lived a long life. I got married to my wonderful soulmate Catherine, we had two lovely children. I built a home. Made a good living. Even made it through the war; although there were some difficult times. Some really difficult times actually, we lost many people close to us. In a strange way, the grief of not having you here was my driving force for building a life of meaning in a world where I felt like a stranger. I have done some amazing things, and met some incredible people as a result.

Now I am coming to the end of my time, but I feel at peace with this. So please also find peace in the knowledge that I have lived a life I am happy with. I've missed you, and I often wondered if I could do something to change dad's fate; but how and who would listen to me? You and dad are not even born yet as write this.

Please live your life. Don't live in the past, live in the present.

Love always,

Patrick Doyle Hunt 1979

Despite Patrick pleading for her not to worry and to continue living her life, she still visits the bridge every morning. Wandering through the meadow, sitting on the farmhouse walls, throwing stick after stick into the stream. Her world had turned into a single episode on constant repeat; reliving the same scenes each day. Every evening Alicia finds herself sitting in Patrick's room, leaving everything exactly as it was. She curls up on his bed and loses track of time, lost in memories as she breathes in the smells and sights of his messy room. Her heart aches terribly.

Her usual visit to the bridge had come and gone, and now she sits staring out of the kitchen window watching the hours tick by. She thinks about Rosheen and Lishy, and how much comfort seeing them has brought; even if the situation is unconventional to say the least. She struck up an instant friendship with Rosheen, much to her own surprise. Rosheen had visited once again, this time with her husband and Lishy. There had been a brief moment of drama when Lishy had decided to play hide-and-seek without informing anyone, and she tucked herself away just behind the bridge. Alicia almost keeled over in fright at the thought of losing another child to the past. She was sure that Rosheen suspected there was more to her story than she had shared, and often caught her observing her reaction to certain topics. Alicia had listened intently to Rosheen describe Patrick as she recalled stories that her grandmother had told her; Alicia's mind was blown by the idea of her 11-year old son being described as an old granddad. Alicia cherished the few stories Rosheen had shared about him. It felt like she had been given a tiny window into his life, and she enjoyed looking through it whenever her grief became too much.

She spots Ali and Rolando walking up the path towards the house. She waves and gestures for them to come straight inside. She has not seen much of them in the last week or so, and she knows they are growing increasingly concerned about her.

'Hey Alicia', Rolando appears through the doorway with his arms outstretched ready to receive a hug.

Ali is not far behind, and places his hand on Alicia's shoulder as he makes his way to the table and sets down a dish of homemade lasagna.

'I made this for you. We need to make sure you're eating', Ali says.

'Thank you', Alicia says, reaching out for Ali's hand.

He carefully places the lasagna in the almost-empty fridge. Rolando pulls out one of the heavy wooden chairs and sits down. Ali remains standing.

'Why don't I make us all a drink?', suggests Ali. He walks over to the cabinet and pulls out three cups.

'How about something a little stronger than tea?', Rolando suggests.

Ali looks at Alicia who smiles and nods agreement.

'Perhaps a little tipple', she says.

Ali heads to the Welsh dresser and opens up one of the display cabinets. As he pulls out a bottle of whiskey he notices an object placed on the bottom shelf. He freezes and stares at it for a moment.

'Alicia is *that* the original stick?', he asks.

She turns towards him, intrigued by his sudden interest in the stick. She had kept it tucked away; for some reason she felt unable to discard it, even though her rational mind still niggled at her whenever she entertained the idea it was magic.

'Er yes', she says.

'The one that broke in two?', he says. '

Yes', replies Alicia, now feeling confused.

Ali slowly reaches down and picks up the stick from the shelf, and he turns towards them in slow motion. He holds the stick up in front of him. It is no longer broken.

They all gawp at it, unsure what to make of this latest conundrum. Their faces full of astonishment.

'Crikey', exclaims Ali.

'Crikey is one word for it', says Rolando. 'Maybe not the word I'd use.'

Alicia leaps up and takes the stick from Ali. She examines it all over; her fingers run over the spot it was broken again and again. It is smooth. No signs of damage at all. *It is definitely the same stick*, she mulls.

'How?', she cries, looking towards Rolando and Ali.

'How is any of this possible? I mean a self-mending stick almost seems expected at this point', Ali says, flabbergasted.

She waves the stick in the air to test its endurance; triple checking it really is no longer broken. Suddenly a loud crashing sound makes them all jump. A spray of shattered glass is strewn across the kitchen floor. Their eyes follow the trail and they spot the photo on the wall has fallen off its hook; the photo of Rhys with his arm around Alicia. She looks at the photo now free from its glass enclosure.

'I've got to go back to the bridge!', she says. 'Now!'

'Why?', asks Ali, taken aback.

Ali carefully tries to navigate his way around the broken glass, moving in such a way it resembles a moonwalk. He reaches over for the dustpan in the corner.

'I have no idea', she replies, her eyes still fixed on the picture.

Rolando and Ali stare at her expectantly; they had anticipated more of an explanation. Looking up at her friends' eager faces she tries to offer some reasoning.

'I mean, if this thing suddenly fixes itself then surely it makes sense to check if the bridge has - fixed itself I mean', Alicia says.

She throws her head back dramatically.

'I think it's safe to say I am making this up as I go along', she adds, sounding exasperated.

Rolando and Ali shrug and nod in agreement, trying to be supportive. Rolando glances at the photo on the floor and then looks up at the intact hook on the wall suspiciously. Both he and Ali wish they could offer up some profound explanation, but they cannot. They are as perplexed as Alicia.

'In that case', says Rolando heading towards the dresser. 'I need some of this first.'

He grabs the bottle of whiskey and takes a swig.

'Rolando!', says Ali in shock.

Rolando shrugs. Alicia cannot help but smile in amusement. After a quick gulp of whiskey, Rolando realises he has made a mistake, as the affects of the alcohol hit him.

'Wait!', Rolando says over-dramatically. 'If it's the stick that's magic then why can't we just use it here. Why the stream and the bridge?'.

Rolando leans against the dresser to steady himself.

'Well, I...', Alicia stutters. 'Well yes that is a good point actually.'

She is not quite sure what to do next though. Alicia stares at the stick like it is the first time she is seeing it; she waves it about and swooshes it around in the air above her. Nothing happens. Ali and Rolando are torn between laughing, or trying to think of a way to activate this seemingly magical object.

'Perhaps it just works with water?', Ali says in desperation.

They all know they are clutching at straws but nevertheless they find themselves being led to bath tub by Rolando. Alicia fills the tub with just a few inches of water.

'This is completely deranged isn't it?', she says turning to her two friends.

'Yes', they both reply in unison.

She drops the stick in. Nothing happens. She places her hand in the tub and begins splashing the water to see if any part of it remains still, like it had done under the bridge. Still nothing happens.

The three friends stare at each other.

'To the bridge then', they all say together.

***

'Can I ask you both something?', Alicia says.

Rolando and Ali are stood either side of her on the bridge. She is poised to drop the stick into the stream. They are a little shocked that she is delaying doing something that she is so anxious to do.

'If I can bring him back, should I?', she asks.

Ali and Rolando stare at her in amazement.

'Having read about the life he has lived. The family he made. I mean, I've met his daughter's daughter. MY great-granddaughter! And my great-great-granddaugher!'

She steps back from the edge of the bridge and looks at her two friends.

'I bring him back, and they no longer exist. Their lives are gone. Poof! Just like that.'

They all stare at each other. Rolando and Ali's mind race with this new information, having not thought about it before now. Alicia's mind feels ready to implode.

'I confess I never even thought about it like that', says Ali finally. 'I mean, he could return here and have an equally amazing life.'

'Or you could join him in 1919', says Rolando.

Ali shoots him a look.

'Well hang on let's not be hasty', Ali says.

'How would I know that me being there in 1919 doesn't alter things? Everything good that has happened to him is because I wasn't there.'

'Everything that was bad could have happened to him also because you weren't there', says Rolando.

The three of them plunge into deafening silence once more.

'I know this will sound odd', Alicia says.

Rolando and Ali laugh; nothing seems odd to them now.

'But', Alicia continues, 'in a way I have been given a gift of sorts.'

She looks at her friends' puzzled faces.

'I mean, every mother worries about what their child's future holds. They hope they will be healthy, live a long life, find happiness. Well…'

Alicia pauses and organises her thoughts.

'I have that knowledge. I know what his life has in store.'

Rolando places an arm around her.

'Time-travel seemed like such a fun idea but in reality it is like someone dumps a 10,000 piece puzzle on you to solve; and you are constantly trying to piece it together as the picture is forever changing', Rolando says thoughtfully.

'Well... I'm sure it could have been interesting', Alicia says. 'If we found a way to stay hidden, talk to no one and interfere with nothing.'

'Sounds fun', Ali says with a slight smirk.

'Oh no and what about the Prime Minister!', Alicia cries, remembering the story Rosheen had told her.

Rolando and Ali look more confused than they have ever been.

'David Cameron?', Ali says. 'I'm not sure how he fits into this.'

'No not that one', Alicia says, shaking her head.

Ali and Rolando look at each other with raised eyebrows. The three friends cease speaking once again, each lost in their own thoughts. The conversation had come to an abrupt and odd end.

'Of course, there is one other thing to consider', Ali says slowly. 'If Patrick, or both you and Patrick, go to 1919 for good - where do we say you've gone?'

Alicia stares back at him unblinking. *Another obstacle to consider,* she thinks to herself.

'I mean, for now it's the summer holidays. But when school returns and there is no Patrick....?', Ali continues.

Alicia nods, feeling exasperated.

'Ultimately I want to give Patrick the best chance in life', she says with an air of regret and sadness. 'And maybe the trade off for that is an uncomfortable one for me.'

Both Ali and Rolando look equally anguished by this statement. Neither of them know what to say in response; instead their silent understanding is enough for Alicia.

'Well we can't stand around here all day', she announces.

She carefully drops the stick into the stream. All three race to the other side and wait. It does not re-emerge. They collectively gasp. *Could it really have worked,* Alicia thinks. She hurries down to the familiar route into the stream and under the bridge. Shoes still on, trousers not even rolled up; the adrenaline is back pounding through her body, egging her on.

Rolando leans into Ali.

'Should we go too?', he whispers.

'Absolutely not', comes Ali's quick reply. 'You'd never survive if you get trapped back there. You struggle enough when the wi-fi goes down.'

Rolando looks affronted but concedes there is some truth in his words. They watch Alicia disappear beneath the bridge.

Stepping out from underneath the arch she looks around her. *Colder and overcast,* she thinks. She blows some air out of her mouth. *Mist.*

'I can't believe that it actually worked', she says to herself with delight.

She edges towards the verge; her heart nearly stops. She spots Patrick in the distance walking away from the bridge. His hair is a little longer, but she knows it is him. Her feet remain frozen to the spot. She wants to scream out his name, but no sound comes out of her mouth. Doubt begins to seep into her thoughts. *What should I do? Stay living in the past with no idea whether Patrick's life will work out the same way. Bring him back to the future and rob Rosheen and Lishy of their lives?*

Alicia did not realise she would find this decision so difficult. She had hoped once she saw him all of the unanswered questions would suddenly make sense; that she would instinctively know what to do. The reality of the situation is quite different to what she imagined.

Patrick is almost out of sight, heading back in the direction of the farmhouse. Alicia watches as he disappears from view. She feels something nudging the side of her shin, and looks down to discover the stick bopping in the water. She bends down and picks it up. She looks back up towards where Patrick was, and back down at the stick. She moves back towards the bridge and props herself up against the wall watching the smoke of the farmhouse rise up on the horizon.

She spots something moving on the bank causing her to jump. As the object comes into focus she is astonished to see the duck staring back at her, no doubt assessing if she has any food to offer.

'Huh', she says. 'I wonder if you are confused by any of this.'

The duck quacks at her. She lets the bridge take the full weight of her body as the minutes tick by. She continues to stare into the distance where she last saw Patrick; undecided what to do for the best.

She raises up the velvet grey stick in front of her and stares at it aimlessly. The more she stares the more her brain pushes her to focus on some marks at the base of the stick. She had not really noticed them before; at a glance they look like nothing more than some random lines. As she draws the stick closer to her eyes the random lines begin to look like recognisable shapes. *They are letters,* she thinks. She squints and tries to trace each mark with her eye to understand the word that is etched on the stick. Then suddenly she realises what is is says. She gasps.

'Eric', she says. 'I knew it! I knew that vanishing whittling man had something to do with this. Ha!'

Two memories violently push their way to the front of her mind, and she almost falls over as the memories smash together and force a clear picture to form in her mind.

'How did I miss this. Rhys is Eric. Eric is Rhys!'

She stares back down at the stick, unsure what to do with this new information. She rubs her head wishing she did not feel so befuddled. Wishing that she had just called out to Patrick, marched him back through to the future with no hesitation. She thought back to her life a month ago; cleaning her house, working through her chores and keeping to her routine had been the backbone of existence. *A simpler time.* But that life was gone. For too long she has tried to control things. *Time to let that Alicia go,* she thinks.

'So', she says to herself slowly. 'My husband was from the past trapped in the future. And my son is from the future with a life mapped out in the past. Unless I choose to change that of course.'

She looks back at the duck.

'What would you do?', she says.

Silly, she thinks to herself. *Fancy asking a duck.* With that, the duck takes flight and disappears in the direction of Patrick. She watches it glide with grace out of view towards the farmhouse.

She pulls out Patrick's letter once again, and begins to read the following words:

... the grief of not having you here was my driving force for building a life of meaning in a world where I felt like a stranger. I have done some amazing things, and met some incredible people as a result.

She knew Patrick had written this to give her comfort, but it was these words that were making her question her next move.

'Maybe I have already made the decision. This letter confirms it. I never went back for him', she says out loud to herself.

'But then again, here I am now with the power to change his future.'

She returns the letter to the safety of her pocket and shakes her head dramatically.

'Time-travel isn't for the weak', she concludes.

Stroking the stick she considers that she may well be holding an object that is the only one of its kind in the entire world. *There's so much more to you than a passageway under a bridge,* she thinks to herself.

Alicia clenches her hands into fists and steadies herself for what is about to happen. The fate of many lives rests on her next decision; and she knew it.

'I know what I must do', she says.

Holding the stick tightly, she begins to move.

-End-

www.e-lowri.com

Printed in Poland
by Amazon Fulfillment
Poland Sp. z o.o., Wrocław
30 July 2023

ebda5a1b-226b-4ae0-8fe2-123fd06ab54dR01